WILD RIDE

POWERTOOLS: HOT RIDES, BOOK #1

JAYNE RYLON

HAPPY ENDINGS PUBLISHING

ABOUT THE BOOK

Can a marriage of convenience turn into true love? Maybe...with the help of the right man.

Quinn has made mistakes—like sleeping with the wrong people. It's taken him time to figure out what he wants in bed and out of it. Understandable, since he's attracted to both men and women and surrounded by a network of friends who seem to have no trouble finding love in any combination.

When he meets Trevon—the sexiest man ever—on the side of the road, only one thing keeps Quinn from pursuing him: Trevon's even sexier wife, Devra.

Like Quinn, Trevon and Devra have led rough lives. Financial and safety concerns forced them into a marriage of convenience they both secretly wish was more.

The lessons Quinn's past taught him should put the brakes on his fantasies of propositioning Trevon and Devra for a one-night ménage. But the need to atone for his previous transgressions, along with pure temptation, drives him to bring the struggling couple closer, even if it means breaking his own heart in the process.

This is a standalone book in the Hot Rides series and includes an HEA with no cheating. The series is part of the greater universe where both the Powertools and Hot Rods books are also set, so you can visit with many of your previous favorite characters and see what they're up to now!

ADDITIONAL INFORMATION

1

"**Y**ou calling it quits already? What the hell am I paying you top dollar for?" Gavyn crossed his arms as he leaned his shoulder against a metal pole in the center of his motorcycle repair and restoration shop, Hot Rides. His words might have sounded harsh, but his crooked smile promised they harbored no true irritation.

"Because I'm the best mechanic in this shop. Even my asshole boss knows that." Quinn smirked up at his very non-asshole boss. Their relationship had more in common with that of siblings than employer and employee. Hell, Gavyn had practically watched Quinn grow up, from a punk fifteen-year-old into...well, a punk twenty-two-year-old.

Not much had changed on that front, really.

Besides, the guy clearly had a soft spot for Quinn, who hadn't even gotten fired yet this week. Although he'd been canned a couple times in the past, Gavyn always rehired him within a few hours. It would be awkward if he didn't, considering Quinn lived in a tiny home on the Hot Rides property that they'd built together after Quinn had graduated high school. That was a perk of being the biological little brother of one of Gavyn's closest friends.

It wasn't just that, though. Quinn had worked his ass off, day in and day out, for the past four years to help the shop grow from a start-up to something they were hardly able to manage between them anymore. Not even with occasional help from the Hot Rods gang, mechanics at their sister shop, which focused on building badass cars.

"Kid, you're the *only* fulltime mechanic at this shop." Gavyn winced.

"See?" Quinn tried to laugh it off though he was stressed and careening toward burnout, which would only make the situation worse. Gavyn counted on him. They were going to have to start turning business down if they didn't figure things out and expand Hot Rides soon. Of course, that only meant more responsibility for him as the shop manager. He had to do something to get his head on straight. Given his family history of alcoholism, downing a few beers wasn't an option.

"I'm taking a late lunch break to go for a ride since my next appointment cancelled last minute. I need a little fresh air. Cool?"

"You know I'm just busting your balls, kid." Gavyn squeezed his shoulder. "Hell, if it wasn't for that inventory count I promised Amber I'd finish today, I'd join you."

"You sure you don't want to blow that off?" Quinn grinned, always willing to be a bad influence. "For some dumb reason, she loves you. She'll forgive you. Especially if you make it up to her later..."

"Don't be thinking about how I smooth things over with my wife. Unlike your brother and the rest of his gang,

I don't share well with others." Gavyn snapped a dirty rag in Quinn's direction, stopping short of actually flicking him with it. Even when roughhousing, none of their friends ever laid an aggressive finger on him. Physical contact—especially the cruel kind—wasn't something to joke around about. Not after what he'd lived through. "Go ahead. Have enough fun for both of us. Just be back in time for your next appointment."

"Yeah. Of course." After all Gavyn, Quinn's brother—Roman—and the rest of their friends had done for Quinn, he would never let them down. They'd literally saved his life, and he would never forget it.

"Probably be best if you eat some fucking lunch while you're on break." Gavyn spread his feet and stood taller then. "You look like you're getting skinnier. Don't make me tell Ms. Brown she needs to feed you. Or maybe I should, so she'll bring a shit-ton of grub over and I can have some, too."

Gavyn's mother-in-law, along with Quinn's brother and the rest of the Hot Rods, had practically raised Quinn after they'd rescued him from his own mother's house of horrors. Ms. Brown could cook better than a chef in a five-star restaurant and he didn't even have to dress in stupid fancy clothes to eat at her house.

Quinn ran his hands down his stomach, feeling the lean muscles beneath his skin. Were they more pronounced? Maybe. Lately nothing had appealed to his...appetites.

He reverted to the Quinn he'd used to be, the one who didn't say much and got hurt so often that he didn't bother to argue when it wouldn't do any good. With a shrug, he turned away from Gavyn and grabbed his helmet.

"Keep the rubber side down. Don't take any

unnecessary risks." Gavyn cleared his throat. "You know, adrenaline is a drug, too."

Quinn for sure wasn't touching that one. Gavyn and Quinn's brother had become fast friends after they'd met in a last-resort rehab facility. They'd struggled with sobriety from drugs and alcohol long enough that they both understood some of his urges. Instead of responding, he put his helmet on, loving how it blocked out the entire world except for what was right in front of him. It would force him to focus on staying between the lines as he flew over the pavement.

That would have to be concession enough to please Gavyn.

Quinn slapped the tinted visor of his helmet down, swung a leg over his motorcycle, and then started it. The engine coming to life between his knees shook the knots from his shoulders. Here he was powerful and in control.

He flexed his fingers, nodded at Gavyn, then took off with a roar that could have come straight from his soul. Freedom. Escape. Whatever you wanted to call it, he lived for it. *Needed* it.

Besides sex, riding was the best relief he could find from the dark thoughts that still haunted him from time to time. Gavyn was right. Exhilaration was his drug of choice. His opportunities for a hit had been limited recently, since he'd been striking out in bed.

Middletown wasn't exactly a mecca for eligible, freaky singles. Nightlife was limited to a few honkytonk bars. And he'd already fucked his way through the more-than-willing women...and guys...around. Sure, he'd gone out prowling at those dives, done some dancing, played a few games of pool, and sat in the corner, watching for anyone who caught his eye. Since he didn't drink—not after he'd experienced firsthand how alcohol had turned his mother into a monster, nearly cost Gavyn his soulmate, and attempted to destroy his own brother—he usually got bored pretty quickly, before he could find anyone interesting to take home.

His reputation didn't help. It frightened the majority of his potential lovers away. He was far too wild a ride for most of the normal folks who lived in their conservative Midwestern town. Quinn wondered if it was the fact that he was bisexual or into the occasional threesome that made a bigger black mark against him. Either way, he was getting pretty fucking tired of having to explain himself or make excuses for the way he'd been built.

It could be he was getting old, like Tom—Ms. Brown's husband and the father figure for all the misfits at Hot Rods and now Hot Rides, too—had recently teased him. Since he'd been forced to grow up quick, he sometimes felt like he was twenty-two going on sixty. Today being one of those days.

As much as he loved Hot Rides and the extended family he hadn't always been lucky enough to have supporting him, he wondered if it might be time to move on and find a place where he could be the man he truly wanted to be, in all aspects of his life. Somewhere urban, where he might be able to discover more unattached people like him.

Problem was, he'd have to understand exactly who he was first.

With a twist of his wrist, Quinn cranked the throttle, hunkering lower as the bike leapt forward. The rear tire fishtailed before he could straighten it out. His heart leapt as he brought his motorcycle under control.

Sorry, Gavyn, he apologized mentally as he did exactly what his friend had told him not to do.

People were right to worry about him.

He raced down a road that got curvier and narrower as he left Middletown behind, if only for a little while. It took miles and miles before he realized his mind had blanked. Gone were the ruminations about how stuck he felt, his responsibilities to Gavyn, what felt like an impending betrayal of his brother and the rest of their friends, his lack of companionship—everything except the vibration in his hands and the heat billowing off the matte black metal beneath him.

A switchback in the road marked the farthest point of his loop. With a sigh, he turned toward home with the restlessness inside him quenched temporarily. He'd already started thinking about what parts to pull for his upcoming service appointment when he spotted a flash of something on the shoulder of the road up ahead.

Another motorcycle. Candy-apple red. Some sort of vintage Indian that had seen much better days. It was in shitty condition, but sexy as fuck nonetheless. Quinn swerved toward it even before he noticed the spectacular jeans-clad ass pointed in his direction as a guy bent over to inspect the broken-down bike. A shirtless, ripped guy with skin the color of rich, oiled walnut. He was sweaty and running his hands over his ultra-close cropped hair as if he was about to lose his shit.

It was exactly the diversion Quinn craved right then.

He licked his lips as he skidded to a stop on the shoulder of the road a little too quickly to say he was complying with Gavyn's command to be careful. Then again, checking out a stranger and his motorcycle on a deserted country road probably wouldn't qualify as safe either.

None of that stopped Quinn from doing it anyway.

2

—————

Quinn tugged off his helmet. He tucked it under his arm, against one hip, as he shook his hair out of his face. He kept it pretty short on the sides, but it always got out of control on top, especially when he was riding. He used the other hand to rake it into some sort of decent order. "Hey. Need a hand?"

The guy cursed under his breath as he unfolded himself and stood.

Quinn backed up a half-step. It wasn't very often he had to look up to someone. Not after that last growth spurt he'd had when he was about nineteen. Hell, of all the Hot Rods, only Bryce was taller than him now.

This man had them both beat by at least four inches. His black polo with a logo for a local landscaper embroidered on the chest was draped around his neck. A bead of sweat rolled from his collarbone, down the flat spot between his pecs then over ab after ab after ab. Damn, manual labor had its benefits.

Suddenly, Quinn felt the need to clear his throat. He licked his lips instead.

"Nah, what I need is a fucking ride that doesn't break down every other day." The guy grimaced. Even the snarl twisting his lush lips couldn't mar his gorgeous face. He was model material—tall, very dark, and pretty much the most handsome example of maleness Quinn had ever seen. "Can't even keep a shitty job when I'm late or calling off all the damn time because of it. Gonna have to give up and sell her."

Damn. That had to hurt. The Indian was a classic. Not something you came across every day, not even in Quinn's line of work.

"It may not be reliable, but it sure is beautiful. What is it, a 1940s Chief?" Quinn sighed as he ripped his gaze from the guy's perfect physique before it could wander below the waistband of his faded black jeans. He didn't care to get himself decked today.

"Close. It's a '38. And thanks." The guy betrayed his frustration by angling away to run a fingertip over the contour of the deep fender.

Quinn was instantly jealous as fuck.

Until the man spun back toward him and stuck out his hand. "I'm Trevon Russell, by the way. Thanks for stopping. Do you have any idea how far we are from Middletown?"

His grip was strong and steady when his long fingers wrapped around Quinn's hand and shook it. "Quinn Daily. About ten miles."

"Shit." Trevon crouched down again and started jiggling things around. "I'm never going to make it if I walk. My boss said I'm done if I'm late again."

Quinn could already tell his efforts were pointless.

"Looks to me like you need a new distributor. The cap is cracked, and with all the rain we've been getting lately..."

He turned his head slightly toward Trevon, taking in the man's thick lashes and his amber eyes speckled with gold from up close. He didn't look any less flawless from a foot away.

"Yeah, the thing's shot." Trevon stood and kicked a rock into the underbrush. "I've patched it up ten times too many. The spark plugs keep getting fouled too."

"Fortunately, I know a kick-ass mechanic." Quinn put his hand over his eyes like a visor and peered up at Trevon, who glared into the woods. His good looks weren't obscured by his hand, which ran over his super-short buzz cut over and over.

Quinn wished he could do that for the guy, soothing him with repeated caresses as they made out. Trevon obviously needed an outlet for his frustration at least as much as Quinn had when he'd left the shop earlier.

Trevon grunted. "Probably expects to get paid then."

"My rates are negotiable. We can work something out." Quinn wouldn't mind sharing a pizza and an evening of the guy's time after a long, hard ride...or maybe before a private one...in exchange for his skills.

"You?" The guy whipped his head around, taking a long look at Quinn's immaculate, custom motorcycle. Was that appreciation sliding in behind the aggravation?

Quinn hoped so. He took a lot of pride in his work. "Yeah. My friend owns the shop in Middletown. Hot Rides. I work there."

Technically he was the head mechanic and Gavyn had made him a partner when he'd given him shares of the business for his twenty-first birthday, but he didn't intend to come off as a pompous asshole when this guy was clearly struggling. Hell, he'd been there before. It was only by the grace of his big brother, Roman, that he'd escaped as whole as he had.

"I've heard of the place. Definitely can't afford it. Thanks, though." Trevon's hand paused its circuit over his head and said, "Maybe, if it's not too much trouble, I could come by and buy a used cap. Maybe something I could modify and make fit, if you've got any junk parts hanging around."

"You've got experience with that?" Quinn asked, impressed.

"Well, kind of. I do the best I can. Watch a lot of videos online and tinker until I get it right. I've been restoring this old thing since my grandfather..."

He trailed off and swallowed hard.

Quinn stared at the motorcycle from where he still crouched in front of it. He put his hand lovingly on top of the perfectly imperfect antique. No wonder Trevon was hanging on to it. Even in this condition, the Indian would be worth a small fortune to the right collector.

He should know, since he dealt with a lot of those daily at Hot Rides.

Quinn was surprised when Trevon plucked his hand from the motorcycle and used the connection to tug Quinn to his feet effortlessly. He wasn't exactly scrawny like he'd been back when his mother's boyfriends had taken their bad attitudes out on him. He didn't hide in attics anymore to avoid confrontation or allow himself to be manhandled, either.

It was kind of hot that Trevon could overpower him like that. Probably because he didn't seem like the kind of guy to abuse that strength. "What do you think, could that work out?"

"Sure. Let me get a tow truck over here from our sister shop. We'll give you a lift to work and then you can come by afterward to see what we can do about the bike. It's no big deal. Rebel is on his way back from delivering a hot rod this afternoon. He's probably going to come right by here any time now."

"I can walk it."

Quinn knew that stubborn set to Trevon's jaw well. A mixture of ego and embarrassment that didn't solve any problems. He knew better than to argue directly. So he tried to be a bit more subtle when what he really wanted was to throw this man to the dirt and fuck the bitterness and resentment right out of him, leaving them both relaxed and happy.

"You could, but that would suck. I think the news said it was going to hit the nineties today. It's no imposition, and I swear I'm not looking to get paid for it either. Bring some pizza with you after work and we'll be cool." Quinn shrugged one shoulder. The words flew from his mouth before he could think better of them. So much for Gavyn's earlier advice about playing things safe. "Better yet, hang out and have a few slices with me before we figure out what's wrong and how to fix it together."

"Did you just proposition me?" Trevon raised a sexy brow. He didn't take a swing at Quinn, though, so that was a good sign. Quinn had learned early to duck when he said shit like that. He should know better by now, considering that he'd been hitting on guys for nearly eight years. Sometimes it was worth the risk.

Life would have been easier if he'd been attracted only to dainty, meek women, or to guys who were significantly less ripped than this one. But hey, it wouldn't be nearly as fun. His heart was pounding twice as hard as it had when he'd been shattering the speed limit a few minutes ago.

"No. I mean, not in the way you're thinking. You don't have to do anything you're not into for me to offer my help. If you're down, though, who knows what I'll service after your bike?" Quinn smiled as if he hadn't just offered to handle the guy's dipstick.

The spark that flashed through Trevon's lion eyes reminded Quinn of the fire that powered an internal combustion engine. Hot. Fast. And heady. So it shocked the hell out of him when Trevon backed up, shaking his head. "Sorry, man. I'm not into that."

Like hell he wasn't.

Quinn signed. If Trevon wasn't ready to admit his desires to himself, it wasn't Quinn's job to force him into accepting them. He held his hands up. "Hey, no problem. But I'm calling the tow truck anyway. You can thank me later."

Trevon sputtered as Quinn fished his cell from his pocket while tracking the other guy's stare straight to the bulge in his well-worn, ripped, and grease-stained jeans. *Not interested, my ass.* He smirked as he punched the icon for one of his favorite contacts. After a single ring, a warm voice said, "Hot Rods garage. How can I help you?"

"Hey Amber! Can you do me a favor?"

His boss's wife, who also managed their sister business —Hot Rods—chuckled. "Quinnigans. What'd you get yourself into this time?"

"Nothing yet." He tried not to sound petulant. "Can you send Bryce over to Route 33 with the flatbed? Near that barn where Meep ran that time my brother was an idiot..."

None of them were about to forget that night. She'd know exactly where he meant.

"Are you okay?" Her teasing tone vanished. "Gavyn said you went out for a ride."

"I'm fine. I didn't wreck or anything like that. I found someone on the side of the road who could use a little help." Quinn glanced up at Trevon, who was digging a trench in the rubble with the toe of his sexy-as-fuck leather boots, his hands fisted.

Quinn couldn't help it. Like a magnet, he was drawn to the guy's bad attitude and that pissed-at-the-world vibe Quinn had worn himself for long enough that he recognized it and wanted to take it away. Like the Hot Rods and the rest of his extended family—Gavyn and Amber included—had mostly done for him.

"Oh! Yeah, of course." Amber would go out of her way for anyone she could help. None of them had led charmed lives, but they'd survived by sticking together. It was one of the things Quinn loved about his quasi-brothers and sisters. "Hold on, let me tell him."

The phone muffled for a second as Amber must have tucked the receiver against her chest and radioed Bryce. She relayed Quinn's location, then came back on the line. "He says he'll be there in ten."

"Thanks. I owe you one." Quinn couldn't help but smile as he realized he'd have a little more time to get to know this guy whom he'd definitely never seen before today. He glanced at his watch, then winced. "Will you tell Gavyn I'll be a couple minutes behind schedule?"

"Call him yourself." She snorted.

"No way. Come on. He's your husband. He won't get mad at you." Quinn's mouth slanted in a wicked grin as he remembered Gavyn's earlier warning when he'd said something similar to his boss-friend.

"Okay, fine." Amber laughed. "This rescue of yours must be pretty cute if you want to wait around with them for Bryce. It's not like you to blow off work."

"You have no idea." Quinn had to stifle a groan. Then he wheezed, "Please."

"Of course. Good luck, Quinnigans." Amber made kissy noises as she hung up on him.

Quinn cleared his throat, jammed his phone in the back pocket of his jeans, then ambled toward Trevon, hoping the other guy couldn't tell how excited he was about their chance meeting. Damn, his life must be pretty boring lately to get this fired up over finding a man on the side of the road, even one as studly as Trevon.

3

Trevon couldn't believe his shit luck. First, his motorcycle died on the way to work. Again. Then he got rescued by the sexiest man he had ever seen outside of a magazine or the movies...including porn. He was cut and tattooed and had piercing blue eyes that made it obvious he saw right through Trevon's faked disinterest.

Maybe it was adrenaline fueling his insane attraction to this stranger. Despite his frustration and the despair of knowing he was going to lose another job, his dick was doing its best to overcome his bad mood and rise to the occasion. Of course, that only made him feel worse about himself and the direction his life was heading in.

Quinn, and all men, were strictly off limits.

Trevon rubbed the back of his neck. His impromptu massage didn't do much to alleviate the knots there or the headache that was starting to cloud his judgment with pain. He couldn't afford to do something stupid.

Thankfully, it really was only a few minutes before a giant tow truck—driven by an even more imposing man with dark hair and shoulders broad enough to look normal in that beast of a vehicle—pulled up beside them. When he opened the door, a black-and-white dog hopped down and raced over to Quinn.

The guy laughed and went to his knees in the dirt to humor the friendly animal. He smothered it in a hug, then petted it over and over until Trevon start wishing he had four legs and a cute bark.

"Trevon, this is Buster McHightops. Oh yeah, and Bryce." Quinn's eyes sparkled as he joked around with his friend, who mumbled and rolled his eyes at the dog and Quinn's antics.

"Nice to meet you. I really appreciate you doing this." Trevon stuck out his hand and shook Bryce's. What the hell was up with the genetics around here?

While Bryce was also handsome as fuck, Trevon kept glancing back at Quinn. There was something more than a pretty face about the guy. It was like he couldn't look away for long.

"It's no problem at all. Shall we go? I heard you're in a hurry." Bryce and Quinn were already rolling the bikes up a ramp onto the flatbed and securing them. They obviously knew what they were doing, so Trevon ambled toward the passenger side of the tow truck.

It was going to be a hell of a ride in there with these two men.

Quinn jogged past and opened the door. He said, "I'll get in first. I don't mind being in the middle."

Bryce poorly disguised a chuckle behind a cough, then climbed into the truck as he made some comment about sandwiches that Trevon was sure he must have heard wrong.

Bryce glanced over at his two passengers. If he noticed

Trevon checking out Quinn's ass as he climbed into the big rig, he was polite enough to pretend not to notice. The guy looked as ferocious as a massive black bear, even if he was acting more like a teddy bear instead.

Trevon eyed the spot on the bench seat that was left for him. Even though the truck was huge, so were the two occupants of the cab, especially with the addition of Buster taking up most of the floorboard. There would be no way to avoid pressing up against Quinn's muscular thigh and brushing their arms together.

If it weren't for his job, he would say fuck it and walk. A man could only resist so much temptation.

Trevon glanced over his shoulder, squinting as if he could figure out a way to fly through the forest to his job site, more than ten miles away.

"Fuck that, kid," Bryce grumbled. "I'm already here. It'll just take us a few minutes to get back to town. It's hot as hell and you're late, remember? I swear Quinn only bites if you beg."

"Yeah. Yeah, okay." Trevon swiped his hand over his mouth, put a hand on the frame of the door, then boosted himself inside. He perched on the edge of the seat, smacking the side of his knee when he slammed the door behind him.

Quinn didn't bother to close his legs when the outside of their thighs pressed together. He probably had giant balls that needed plenty of room. *Don't. Think. About. That.*

Trevon scooted over so that he was plastered against the door and window.

Bryce dropped a hand between him and Quinn. Out of the corner of his eye, Trevon caught the guy flicking Quinn in the ribs. Quinn whipped his head toward Bryce, who widened his eyes in a clear sign for "cut it out".

Trevon finally released his held breath when Quinn tucked his knees together a bit. He gripped the door handle as if they were flying down a twisty mountain road at two hundred miles an hour rather than trundling toward town. Every dip and jolt caused him to bump into the rippling muscles of Quinn's leg, arm, and side.

Quinn was grinning while Trevon tried not to flinch. It was either that or he'd make more of a fool of himself than he already had today.

"So where are we dropping you off?" Bryce asked as Buster McHightops curled up at Trevon's feet.

"I'm part of the landscaping team working on the new golf course and the attached housing development off Henderson." Or at least he hoped he still was.

"That place is huge." Quinn whistled. "Fancy too."

"Yup." That single site would provide months of employment. It was hard labor, but as long as it was an honest living, he didn't mind. Ninety days and he could be in a much better place than he was today, if he was careful. "I bet your job is a hell of a lot more fun, though."

For the next few minutes, Quinn talked about how lucky he was to do something he loved. Trevon envied him. For lots of reasons. The shop. His friends. His freedom to look at a guy the way he was looking at Trevon —with heat, and desire, and intention.

Trevon might look, but he couldn't ever have.

He tried not to be bitter about all the things life hadn't handed him, considering some of the amazing stuff it had. They pulled up to the golf course construction entrance before he could remind himself of what those good points were.

Trevon gave Buster one last pat, smiled at Quinn, then hopped down from the tall truck and said, "Thanks again.

I'll be by as soon as I can to figure something out about my bike."

"Take your time." Quinn waved him off. "It'll be safe at the shop until you're ready. Call us if you need a ride."

Trevon nodded, gratitude choking the rest of what he wished he could express. It had been a while since there had been anyone else on his side. Quinn's support gave him the courage to face his boss. Speaking of the asshole...

"What the hell do you think you're doing?" asked Vance, the owner of the landscape company Trevon had been busting his balls for at minimum wage.

Trevon tugged his uniform shirt, which he'd mostly avoided getting too sweaty before the start of his shift, over his head then spun to face the guy. He hadn't even had time to shut the tow truck door before Vance ripped into him. "You might as well take that right back off. You no longer work here, buddy."

"Vance, I'm sorry." Trevon pointed to his motorcycle on the back of the flatbed. "I had—"

"Yeah, I know. Problems with your bike. Same as every other time. Look, you're a hard worker, but I have to have people I can rely on. I told you before, you were on your last shot."

"These guys are helping me get the problem resolved, permanently. I won't be late again."

"I've heard that before. Next time it'll be something else. No. You're done. You're fired. Get out of here." Vance turned his back and walked away as if he hadn't stolen the last shred of hope Trevon had for a better future. Without even his shitty job, he was done for. Sunk.

This had been his last chance.

And he'd blown it.

"Fuck!" he shouted at the sky and the blinding sun beating down on him.

"Come on, Trevon. You don't need to beg that dirtbag to be his indentured servant." Quinn's kind, patient voice held a note of simmering anger. On Trevon's behalf? "Get in the truck. We'll go fix your bike so you can find someplace better to work instead."

Absolute humiliation and shame washed over Trevon. His most desperate moment had been witnessed by a young, sexy, successful man. Precisely what he needed to make it even more horrifying. Maybe this was a nightmare.

He pinched himself.

It hurt. Though not as bad as the rest of his life was going to after this.

"He's right. You don't need this shit. Get in," Bryce said. "Come with us."

Trevon wished he could muster enough pride to turn them down. To tell them he'd be perfectly fine and mean it. But...he couldn't lie like that. So with slumped shoulders, he flung himself into the tow truck and shut the door, quietly this time. He stared out the window at the receding job site until it vanished, just like his prospects of getting his life together.

As if he could sense the utter misery and devastation eating Trevon from the inside, Buster climbed into his lap and laid his head on Trevon's thigh with a whimper. Trevon kept himself from imploding by scratching the dog behind his ear.

What the hell was he going to do now?

Take these guys up on their kindness, fix his bike, then try again to make things right for the people depending on him. That's what. That was the only option he had.

4

Quinn ached for Trevon. He wanted to hug the guy and tell him things would be fine. Maybe kiss the shit out of him until he perked up. But from the stormy look on Trevon's face, Quinn figured there was more to his story. Stuff that might not be as easy to fix as a busted distributor cap.

Quinn's appointment was routine maintenance, something he'd never really considered a luxury until he saw what Trevon was dealing with over in the next bay. Maybe it had been a few years too many since Quinn had started being pampered. He'd begun to lose touch with reality and forget how harsh the world could seem when you were struggling to survive.

Maybe some of his boredom lately had been a serious case of first-world problems.

Quinn felt guilty. How had he lost track of where he'd come from so easily?

The least he could do was help Trevon get over a few of the speed bumps in his path, like Roman and Tom and the rest of the Hot Rods had done for him. He set the fuel filter he'd just removed down on a pile of rags and looked over at Trevon as he took the new one out of its box.

The guy had removed and disassembled the Indian's distributor, the spark plugs, and the surrounding systems. He had everything laid out in neat rows on the bench nearby and was cleaning each component, piece by piece. He was fast and efficient. For someone who supposedly had no official training or apprenticeship, he knew his way around his bike.

Still, Quinn didn't think it was too egotistical to assume he knew even more. After all, he'd been learning from the best mechanics in the state for years now.

"You know, I'd be happy to take care of that for you as soon as I'm done with this." Quinn tucked a rag in his back pocket, then jacked his thumb in the direction of the motorcycle in his bay. "I'm sure Gavyn's got something out back we can use to hold you over until you get a new one."

Trevon cleared his throat. He swallowed, hard, then said, "I have a better idea. If you don't mind me poking around in the scrap heap or using your tools, I can do it myself."

Quinn didn't think that was a better idea at all. He was hoping to spend a few more hours with the guy, and if Quinn didn't help him out, he'd have no excuse to stick around and share that pizza they'd discussed earlier. But still, he shrugged. "Help yourself."

Truth be told, it was kind of a bitch to replace the distributor and all the related parts on those vintage Indians. Odds were that Trevon would need assistance to finish the job. Besides, Quinn didn't want to take anything away from Trevon, after he'd already had such a shitty day. He knew the value in having a purpose. Working at

Hot Rods and now Hot Rides had boosted his confidence and reminded him that he was worth something no matter what he'd been told growing up.

"Thanks, man. I really appreciate it." Trevon left the garage on a mission. For the first time since he'd gotten canned, he stood straight. Quinn watched his long-legged stride until he turned the corner. Damn, he was fine.

Although Quinn worked quickly and efficiently during his service appointment, he couldn't help but peer over his shoulder to spy on Trevon in action. The guy was no stranger to the garage. He found three different distributor caps that were in the ballpark of his old one and began to file one down until it seemed snug. He used some of the metalworking tools, with the safety gear, and created or refined the threads.

Sparks flew across the garage. And not only the ones caused by Trevon's craftsmanship.

Damn. Quinn was hooked. Addicted to the sight and sound of someone else in the shop. And that was even before he took an extra few moments to note how the guy's arms bulged as he cranked the wrench or admire the curve of his tight ass as he bent over.

When someone kicked his boot, Quinn jumped like the stray cat that had been hanging around lately when Buster McHightops chased it.

Gavyn hovered over him with a knowing grin. "You're being obvious."

"Don't know what you're talking about." Quinn wiped imaginary sweat out of his eyes and returned his focus to the job at hand.

Gavyn crouched down beside Quinn and lowered his voice. "Too bad. Because I'm not into guys and even I'm having a hard time looking away. He knows what he's doing."

"Seems that way, yep." Quinn tried not to pout. Trevon clearly didn't need his help. Would have been nice to save the day for someone else for once. He'd had enough of being the little brother, the runt, the guy with no friends and the only unattached member of their gang.

"Also seems that you might not mind if he hung around for a while. What's his deal?" Gavyn asked. "Bryce told me that dickhead Vance fired him. Is that true?"

"Yup." Quinn winced. It had been hard to watch. Only Bryce's grip on his knee had kept him from tearing out of the truck to defend Trevon or kick Vance's ass. Either would have been better than the sick, helpless feeling that had swamped him as he witnessed the devastation in Trevon's eyes upon hearing the verdict.

"So maybe we could snatch him up for the shop. Looks like he could use the cash. And we need another set of hands around here. It seems like people come into our lives at just the right time for just the right reason…"

Quinn knew Gavyn was thinking about his wife, Amber. But why not? This could be a similar situation. He sat up and grinned. "You're a genius."

"You'd be smarter too, if all your blood wasn't detouring south of your brain." Gavyn smirked, then grew serious. "That's not going to be a problem, is it? Working with someone you have the hots for?"

"I can control myself." Quinn hoped he wasn't lying. He'd never wanted someone as bad as he wanted Trevon, and that was only after a few hours of knowing the guy. Maybe the effect would wear off, but he wasn't counting on it.

Gavyn nudged Quinn's shoulder. "Then hire him before someone else snaps him up."

"Don't you want to do it?" Quinn tipped his head. "It's your garage."

"You're the shop manager. Hiring people is your job." Gavyn grinned. "Besides, if he's as grateful as I think he might turn out to be, you could use some points in your favor."

Fuck yes, he could.

"First, wrap this up." Gavyn pointed at the bike. "Mr. Bosch is waiting."

"I'm on it." Especially now that Quinn realized the sooner he finished with the appointment, the sooner he could get started with Trevon.

He tightened the last bolt, then looked toward the workstation where Trevon had set up his stuff—only to find the guy staring in his direction. When Quinn busted him, he jerked, then spun around to stare out at the trees behind the open garage bays.

Thank God Quinn hadn't been imagining things. Chemistry was not going to be a problem between them.

Quinn cleaned up and walked the motorcycle up front to where Gavyn was chatting with Mr. Bosch. He waved so they would know it was good to go. Then he pivoted on the heel of his boot and tried to act casual as he approached Trevon and the antique bike, which Trevon had mostly reassembled by now.

"Looks like you're making some progress." Quinn checked out Trevon's handiwork. It was quality shit. Considering how fast he'd done it and the limited materials he'd had to work with, Quinn was seriously impressed. And he had high standards in the garage.

And in bed.

Trevon would fit in well either place.

Don't be a perv, he lectured himself. Offering Trevon the job had nothing to do with his killer good looks or the seductive pull that seemed to keep drawing them together. Business first, pleasure after.

"Here's the real test." Trevon swung his leg over the motorcycle, then flipped on the engine. It roared to life on the first try, without a single misfire.

"Nice work, man." Quinn held out his fist and Trevon bumped it. Trevon grinned for the first time since they'd crossed paths on the side of the road. Only then did Quinn realize how tense and upset the guy had been.

He really needed some help.

"Thanks. I would have been up a creek without you and your friends." Trevon smiled then. The transformation was glorious. His teeth were white and straight and his mouth was downright enticing with lush lips. His eyes crinkled a bit at the edges like he used to do it a lot, even if he didn't so much lately. "You have no idea how much you saved my ass today."

Oh, saving his ass wasn't exactly what Quinn had in mind.

"You did a lot of that yourself. All I did was give you a ride, a place to work, and a few tools." Quinn shrugged. "I have to say, I'm really impressed with what you've done here. It's the caliber of work we expect from Hot Rods and Hot Rides."

"Shit. That's a hell of a compliment. I don't really watch TV, but I've caught a few episodes of the *Hot Rods* reality show. Those guys are master craftsmen."

Quinn couldn't agree more. His brother and their friends were everything he aspired to be, both personally and professionally. They would know how to bring someone onboard without stuttering or looking like a fool. He channeled Eli, the Hot Rods garage owner, and thought back to how he'd been offered a position in their ranks. Straightforward, and honest appreciation. Those things had won him over. So he gave it a shot.

"What I'm trying to say is your skills were being wasted at the fucking golf course. Since I know you're available, and I'm hoping you'd like to do more of this... we're hiring." Quinn pointed at the bike. "I couldn't have done that any faster or better myself."

"You're..." Trevon blinked a few times. "Seriously? You'd give me a job? Here?"

"Yeah. You've already shown me you can handle it. We've been slammed lately. Too busy for Gavyn and me to keep up, even with Alanso coming over from Hot Rods to help out when he can." Quinn kicked back, ankles crossed as he leaned against a giant tool chest. He pretended like it was casual conversation when he asked, "So are you new to Middletown? Planning on sticking around a while? If so, why not give this a try?"

Obviously, he'd never seen this man around town. He would have noticed an ass like that or a smile that could melt his insides from twenty feet away.

"I...uh... Maybe." Trevon rubbed his temples. "I don't have a lot of options at the moment and I didn't think that was really a possibility but...yeah. That could work."

"Great. If you've got a few minutes, I can call Gavyn's wife, Amber, to bring over one of our contracts. To be honest, we just copied the ones from Hot Rods since they already have their shit together. It should be standard stuff. We pay well. Have decent benefits and shit." Quinn grinned, getting more excited by the minute at the prospect of having someone his age to talk shop with and hang out with and...maybe more with.

This could be exactly what he'd needed to spice things up. So it floored him when Trevon didn't immediately accept his offer.

"Could you give me an hour or two? I need to talk to Devra about it first." Trevon's eyes glazed. He winced as he stared out the open garage door again. Quinn didn't think his fascination had anything to do with the sunlight pouring in there.

"Sure. Who's Devra?" he wondered aloud. Was that a guy's name or a girl's?

Trevon choked. He had to clear his throat three times before he mumbled, "She's my wife."

5

Fuck my life. Quinn's gaze flew to Trevon's ring finger. Had he missed the signs? No. No dent and definitely no gold band. Still, he tried to act like he hadn't just been gutted when he said, "Take your time deciding. You know where to find me when you figure out what you want to do."

He was talking about the shop and the job offer, which he wouldn't dare rescind simply because of the guy's relationship status. It didn't really sound like it in his mind, though. His statement seemed kind of pervy and a whole lot of shady. Because he was asking himself, why? *Why is he married? To a woman? Does she know he's into guys? At least as into me as I am into him? Maybe he sleeps around on her?*

Quinn turned away then, rubbing down the length of his throat to keep the bile from pouring out his mouth at how disgusting he was being. He knew himself that being bisexual didn't have anything to do with loyalty or faithfulness and Trevon had done everything possible to avoid contact in the car earlier. So what if he was attracted to men or even Quinn specifically? That didn't mean he planned to do anything about it.

Bitter disappointment caused Quinn's ugly, knee jerk reaction. It had been—well, forever—since he'd had that kind of chemistry with someone. He'd never experienced the kind of connection he thought they could have had.

Could have.

Because although he was freaky as fuck, he had limits. Violating commitment and trust between people related to each other by blood or marriage was one of them, ever since he'd fucked up. Hormones, lack of self-control, and youth had all been contributing factors. He'd ended up sleeping with his prom date's brother in high school. Thankfully Amy had forgiven him eventually, and they still hung out from time to time today.

He'd nearly wrecked that friendship along with the mostly innocent relationship they'd had. Sure, they never would have lasted. It hadn't been that serious between them, but still...he could have caused permanent damage to her and her family.

Ever since, he'd chosen his partners wisely.

They were usually people he had no attachment to, and people he disentangled himself from before things could get messy. Now the hottest man he'd met was attracted to him. And also married. *Fuck my life.*

"You can change your mind if you want," Trevon said quietly.

"And lose out on a rising star for Hot Rides? No thanks." Quinn forced himself to face Trevon with a smile. "Sorry, it's just that you surprised me. Maybe I was reading things wrong."

At least Trevon didn't deny the instant heat that had flared between them. "Sometimes things don't go as you expect in life and you do the best you can with what you've been given. That doesn't mean you don't love what you've got. It just means it might not have been what you chose for yourself. I mean, take you for example. You've got an immaculate, custom-built bike, you're the manager of a nationally renowned shop, and you're surrounded by friends. You might not be rich, but you're better off than me, and you've got all the stuff that counts in life. Yet you were out there this afternoon driving around like you were lost. Like something is missing and the only way you can find escape—freedom from your demons—is by riding. Weren't you?"

Quinn owed it to him to be honest since he was digging so deep. "Yeah."

"Don't worry, I won't say anything. I only suspected as much because I do it too." Trevon looked him dead in the eye then. "We all have our shit to deal with. I won't judge you for yours if you give me the same respect."

"Fair enough." Quinn couldn't believe Trevon had discerned that much about him in a few short hours. All of it exactly right, too. "So go talk to your wife. See what she thinks."

"Okay. I'm going to take this for a test drive. If I can make it to the café downtown where Devra's hanging out, waiting for me to...get off work from another job I've lost, I'll explain everything that happened today and come back as soon as possible." Trevon shook his head a little, as if he couldn't believe he'd lucked into this situation. He blinked, then jammed his hand out toward Quinn. "Thank you. For everything. This is a huge opportunity for me. For us."

For a second, Quinn simply stared at Trevon's talented hands taking note of the nicks on his knuckles and the calluses marring the slightly lighter skin on his palm, which proclaimed Trevon was a hard worker. He was afraid to even make contact briefly enough to shake because it would be tempting to yank Trevon toward him and kiss him the way he craved.

But then he figured it would be too weird if he didn't accept the gesture, so he tried to smile like he wasn't more disappointed than that time his mom had discovered his secret stash of money—which he'd hoarded from recycling her beer cans—and spent it on a bottle of cheap vodka. It had taken him months to squirrel away a few bucks and he'd been hoping to treat himself to a couple slices of pizza on his birthday. Instead, he'd ended up with a black eye from Missy's backhand when she'd realized he'd been keeping it from her.

He blinked the bad memories away.

Quinn grasped Trevon's warm hand to chase off the chill in his heart. He knew what it was like to have someone help you climb out of a miserable situation. One you never could have escaped on your own. If he could do that for this guy, he'd be happy to, even if he didn't get to ease some of his own loneliness in the process. Hell, just because they weren't making out didn't mean he wouldn't enjoy some company while working at Hot Rides.

Sure, he loved his job, and Gavyn was like another older brother, but...

He needed a gang of his own like Eli had formed at Hot Rods. A crew, like the Powertools had. Or even just a ride-or-die like Ms. Brown had become for Tom.

Otherwise, he was always going to be the odd man out. The annoying little kid leeching off his big brother and his friends. Maybe Trevon could be the start of that. It would beat talking to the bikes while he worked on them, anyway.

Trevon's voice sounded husky when he retracted his hand and said, "I'll be back as soon as I can. I promise."

"No rush." Quinn's smile was genuine this time. "You know where to find me when you make a decision."

6

It wasn't more than an hour before Quinn heard the uneven rumble of Trevon's better-days ride climbing up the long, twisty driveway to Hot Rides. Hopefully that was a good sign. He wondered about Trevon's old lady and whether she realized he was attracted to men as well as women.

Not his pasture, not his bullshit, Quinn reminded himself.

He was wiping his hands on a rag as he went out to meet the guy halfway, hoping for good news. He looked like every dirty dream Quinn had ever had speeding up to the garage with a woman on the back of his motorcycle. Maybe it was because Trevon was so big, but she seemed tiny. Raven hair with a slight blue cast whipped behind her as she clung to her husband.

Why hadn't he guessed? She was going to be every bit as beautiful as the man Quinn had met earlier. Of course she was.

Trevon killed the motor, then held the bike steady as Devra climbed off before joining her in crossing the last several feet to the open garage door. It had been a long time since Quinn worried about what anyone else thought, but he desperately hoped she liked what she saw as she glanced around the giant bays and the machinery inside Hot Rides.

Maybe even when she looked up at him with a reserved smile.

"Trevon, good to see you again." Quinn met them where the blacktop turned to concrete. He was grinning despite his nervousness. He couldn't help it when Trevon was beaming right back. His momentum propelled him forward, his outstretched hand clasping Trevon's again while his other came around to clap the guy on his solid shoulder.

When he pulled back, he noticed Trevon's smile had gone weak. He swiped a bead of sweat from his forehead. Had his discussion with his wife not gone as he'd planned after all?

"Are you going to introduce me?" Quinn tipped his head.

It gave him the opportunity to really get a good look at Mrs. Devra Russell.

Where Trevon was dark, she was golden. All that long, thick black hair framed a face with petite features. The best of which was her eyes. Their unusual shape, accented by bold liner, made them alluring. Her skin was flawless and more earthen than pink. The way she carried herself —with dignity and strength that dared him to make the mistake of judging her based on her slight stature—made him envision her as the warrior queen of some desert land, and him as the favorite concubine in her harem... but he probably shouldn't.

Together, Trevon and Devra were easily two of the

most beautiful people he'd ever seen. The world's finest duo. What were the odds of that?

Quinn knew better than most that bonds forged by circumstances were stronger than those of blood, but something about the way Trevon clasped Devra's hand over his bicep as they neared made him sure they were in this—and all things life threw at them—together. Devra hooked two fingers through Trevon's belt loop, then glanced up at Quinn from beneath long, curled lashes.

Without a hint of intimidation, but rather with a fierce possession, she spoke for Trevon. "I'm Devra. His wife."

Did Trevon often forget to mention that last tidbit, or did she feel the need to remind Quinn because she could tell he had a thing for her mate?

Either way, he had to be careful. He wasn't a home wrecker, and he really could use Trevon's help at the shop.

Quinn retreated a step or three, jamming his hands in his pockets as he rocked backward onto the heels of his boots. Well, shit. "Nice to meet you."

"Same," she said with a smile that softened her. It sounded like she meant it, too. He thought he detected the hint of an accent in her tone, but when she spoke so little, it was hard to tell for sure.

"You know what we were talking about before?" Quinn asked Trevon, forcing a smile through clenched teeth. "Your bike might be a mess, but you're one lucky son of a bitch."

"I wouldn't exactly put it that way," Trevon mumbled under his breath.

Devra snapped her gaze to him then frowned. Her perfect posture wilted.

Quinn arched a brow, but Trevon had already turned away to reassure his wife that everything was fine.

Except it wasn't. Their illusion was shattered in that moment.

Something was fucked up here, more fucked up than Quinn lusting after a married man and his equally married wife. But he wasn't about to get tangled up in their affairs.

"Have you two made a decision?" Quinn wondered. It would probably be easiest if they said they'd agreed to pass. But that would also be boring, and lonely. He held his breath as he turned toward Trevon.

"When I started to tell Devra about the position you offered me, I realized I probably didn't ask enough questions." Trevon cleared his throat. "I mean, about the pay and hours. Plus if I take the job, I'll need to look for somewhere to stay that's close enough that I can walk to work because...well, you've seen my ride. And places around here are mostly houses. Pretty big ones."

Quinn hadn't been privileged his whole life. What now seemed like a modest neighborhood to him would have seemed like castles once, too. He understood the guy and his worries.

He had an idea, and hoped Gavyn wouldn't mind that he offered.

"Uh, yeah. Sorry, I'm not used to hiring people." Quinn smiled at Devra and Trevon, wondering idly how stunning their kids would be. Damn. Was it any wonder his brains were scrambled? He had to get it together. "The position would be full time. All our mechanics at Hot Rods and here make the same amount. Five an hour over union wages."

"That's...great." Trevon's eyes widened and he stood a little taller.

"Well, yeah. But, that's not all. The Hot Rods built

their shop into what it is today because they're invested in it." Quinn found it easy to talk about the shop. It had been his life for four years now. "We follow the same model."

"We don't have any cash for that kind of thing." Devra nibbled her lower lip and clenched Trevon's arm, gently tugging him back toward the bike.

"Not that sort of investment." Quinn stopped her before she could bite a hole in herself. Especially since he couldn't kiss it and make it better. "What I mean is that for every year you work at the shop you get an ownership bonus. Shares in the garage."

"For the mechanics?" Trevon tipped his head. "Seriously?"

"Everyone who works here gets a piece of the profits. Hell, even when I was just sweeping the floor at Hot Rods, they cut me in. We're a family." So it said a hell of a lot that both he and Gavyn had been willing to take Trevon in right away. There was something about him that Quinn wanted.

For the shop, he clarified mentally. Wanted for the shop.

Right.

"That's unbelievably generous." Devra nudged Trevon in the ribs as if telling him to take the job before Quinn changed his mind.

But he had one more thing to sweeten the deal. He couldn't say what made him do it except that he saw in these two people some reflection of the kid he used to be. On the verge of losing it all. They clearly could use some help and he was in a position to pay it forward. Finally.

Maybe it made him feel better about himself, or maybe he was actually doing the right thing like his brother had. But he said, "There's a tiny home out back. My brother, the rest of the Hot Rods mechanics, Gavyn, and I built it several years ago with some help from our friends who own a construction crew. After living in it a while I had some ideas about how to improve the design for what I like and built a second one. The first one is mostly storage, and guests sometimes stay there. It's nothing fancy, but it has all the essentials. If you help me clean it out, you're welcome to live there."

He stopped himself short of saying *rent free*. The scared kid buried inside him reminded him how much it had meant to him to earn his keep at Hot Rods. He wasn't trying to emasculate Trevon in front of his wife.

"How much would the rent be?" Trevon asked.

"Four hundred a month is probably fair. You'll see, it's called *tiny* for a reason. It's not luxurious. But it is cozy and your commute would be pretty damn short." Quinn smiled. "Feel free to bargain with me if you think it's worth less."

"We don't even need to see it." Trevon looked at Devra, who nodded emphatically, making her thick hair swirl around her. "We'll take it. The house and the job."

In that instant, Quinn's suspicions that they didn't have a lot of options were confirmed.

Damn. What was their deal?

Curiosity ate at him, warring with the side of his brain that screamed it was none of his damn business and that he shouldn't get involved in their personal matters. That was going to be kind of hard with them living a hundred feet away and Trevon working with him all day, though.

"What he means to say is *thank you*." Devra hugged Trevon, squeezing the shit out of him. Quinn did his best not to be jealous. Yeah, right.

Then she dashed toward Quinn and flung her arms

around him, too. She rose up on her tiptoes while dragging him down at the same time to kiss his cheek.

She murmured, "Thank you," against his ear before returning to Trevon's side.

Trevon wrapped her in an enormous bear hug and spun her around. Her feet kicked as both of them laughed like they'd won the lotto.

Quinn tried to keep his cock from getting fully hard, but it was no use. Thankfully, the gray jumpsuit he wore over his jeans hid a lot.

This was going to be an awkward situation. But his male role models had taught him that doing what was right was far more important than doing what was easy and this was obviously one of those situations.

He knew it even before Trevon lowered Devra to the ground and she buried her face in Trevon's shirt to hide her sniffle. She knuckled moisture from the corner of her eye as stealthily as possible before beaming up at Trevon, who grinned.

The love between them was obvious, even if they hadn't officially kissed to seal the deal. They cared for each other deeply. Quinn could see it clearly and tried not to be too envious of their bond.

From the doorway, Gavyn whistled. "Now that's what we need more of around here. Welcome to the team."

After some congratulations and ice-breaking conversation, Quinn encouraged the couple to go take a look at the cottage that was their new home. He stayed behind with Gavyn, needing some space to absorb what had just happened as much as the couple did.

When they'd left earshot, holding hands as they walked excitedly toward their new home, Gavyn ruffled

Quinn's hair. He said, "They needed that. You did good, kid."

"We'll see." This had the potential to be amazing or a disaster for the shop and for him personally. He could only hope it turned out for the best.

"You had a thing for him right away, didn't you?" Gavyn asked quietly.

"Doesn't matter."

"She's a good match for him." Gavyn grunted. "Both sexy, and sort of sweet. Very corruptible. They seem like... exactly your type."

Quinn wasn't sure he could have pinpointed what his type was. At least not until he'd met Trevon and Devra. Now he admitted to himself that Gavyn was right.

He spun and kicked his toolbox, his boot leaving a dent in the side of the red metal.

"What the hell are you going to do about that mess?" Gavyn asked.

"Absolutely nothing." Quinn waved his hands. "I don't fuck around with people's relationships. You know that."

"Too bad. They're both smoking hot and seemed to be staring at you plenty when they thought they could get away with it." Gavyn shrugged. "You never know what they're into."

"That's their business. And their problem." Quinn slammed his toolbox closed, then threw his dirty rag in the hamper. "I'm going over to Hot Rods for a couple hours."

Hanging out with his brother and the close-knit gang of mechanics would remind him how precious those sorts of bonds were and why he absolutely couldn't do anything to ruin the one Devra and Trevon had forged between them.

"Good plan. I heard Ms. Brown was making her famous barbeque chicken mac and cheese for dinner."

As if he needed another reason to duck out for a while. Quinn couldn't resist Ms. Brown's cooking. "You coming?"

"Hell yes." Gavyn and Quinn were on their bikes and halfway to Hot Rods before Quinn realized he probably should have told Trevon and Devra where he was going and when he'd be back. It would be weird to get in the habit of having other people around, though it could be good, too.

He debated turning around to tell them but then wondered if they'd be busy christening the tiny house. It was damn uncomfortable to ride his motorcycle with a full-on boner, so he left them to their own devices and concentrated on the delicious meal waiting for him instead.

It would have to be enough to satisfy him, for now.

7

For all of the fifteen glorious minutes it took for everyone to gather around the picnic tables under the pavilion the Powertools crew had built the Hot Rods for Christmas last year and pile their plates with ooey-gooey carbs, Quinn was distracted from the Mr. and Mrs. Russell situation developing at home. He should have realized his nosey-ass family wouldn't leave him alone for long, though.

"So, tell us more about this guy you rescued earlier." Carver, his brother's husband, accented his demand with the roll he held in his hand, about to stuff in his face.

"His name is Trevon. He rides an antique 1938 Indian Chief that's in need of a new distributor, and just about every other part on it." Quinn tried to keep a straight face as he very intentionally avoided telling them how gorgeous the man—and his wife—were. "But he fixed it himself while I was taking care of my afternoon schedule. In fact, he did such a good job of it that Gavyn told me to hire him. So I did. He's moving into my original tiny home. I guess that means we're neighbors."

His next bite of Ms. Brown's famous barbeque chicken mac and cheese got stuck in his throat. He took an enormous pull from the glass of ice water in front of him, draining the whole thing.

"Whoa." Tom nodded from the head of the table. "That's great news. You two have been working your asses off lately. Alanso, too. It's time to expand. I've been saying that for over a year now."

While there were plenty of murmurs of agreement and heads nodded, these people knew him far too well to let him get away with such a clinical description. Even the mention of a rare vehicle wasn't enough to keep them from lasering in on his private life. Most times he didn't mind.

Today...well, he was still a little bitter.

"Is that going to be messy?" Roman wondered. Figured his brother would get to the point. He was too intuitive for his own good sometimes. Or maybe they were more similar than he realized sometimes.

"Being a mechanic usually is." Quinn shrugged, hoping they'd take the hint. He didn't want to talk about it.

"Quit that shit." Holden plopped down on his other side. "It's not like you to be evasive when it comes to people you want. What's up?"

"It's messy as fuck, okay? Trevon is married. He brought his wife with him." He might as well save them some time and spill all the beans. "She's also gorgeous and, obviously, equally off limits."

"Ouch." Holden put his arm around Quinn's shoulder and squeezed before returning his attention to his dinner.

"Yeah." Quinn dropped his head back. There was no reason not to come clean. Between all of them, they might as well have been the fucking Scooby-Doo gang. They found out everything eventually. "I was planning on making a move before I knew that little factoid."

"Oops." Kaelyn, Bryce's wife, wrung her hands. "Are you freaking out about that? I mean, Bryce told me nothing happened on the ride back to town. Just because you thought about it doesn't mean you crossed any lines."

"No. And I won't with either of them, now that I know. I'm capable of keeping my hands, and other parts, to myself." Quinn had no doubts about that. He'd nearly fucked up a close personal relationship once before, when he'd been young and foolish. He wasn't about to let his dick get him in that kind of a mess again.

"But he's going to be working with you. If there's an attraction..." Sally tried to warn him. She should know. She had worked at Hot Rods with Eli and Alanso, her two husbands, for years before they'd gone from friends to lovers. Being near them daily without showing them how she felt had tortured her. And them.

But that was different. Quinn had barely met Trevon and Devra. He didn't even know them. It was just a physical attraction, that's all. Not love. Simple lust.

"There was a spark, sure." He adjusted himself—both the way he was sitting and his junk, which was uncomfortably riled despite the lecture he'd given himself a hundred times in the past several hours. "That doesn't mean I have to do something about it. I'm not sixteen anymore. I know better."

"Not every situation is black and white," Nola pointed out. Her husband, Kaige, nodded in agreement without pausing his fork-to-mouth motion.

"You're grown enough now to understand life isn't always simple." Roman knocked his shoulder into his little brother's. "Hell, you had to learn that early. So maybe this time you need to go slow, careful, and navigate the situation with finesse instead of a sledgehammer. Maybe the results will be different."

"Nah. They're married. A couple. They don't need any intruders. That's that." Quinn dropped his head in his hands, his food suddenly unappealing.

"Is it?" Sally's caustic tone drew his gaze. Uh-oh. What had he said?

Quinn mentally rewound his words. *Oh. Right.*

"Tell that to Eli. I mean, technically I'm married to Alanso. That doesn't mean shit." Sally glared. "I love them both equally. More every day. Although that's not how things started between us all, that's how it is now. They hooked up first. Don't you dare tell me I should have been satisfied that they were happy and walked away from them when I knew how much better we could be as a threesome."

"Technically...." Alanso said, his Cuban accent intentionally heavy. "You did. Well, you drove really fast, crying to the Powertools. But I wasn't about to let you escape that easily. Sometimes you have to fight for what you really want. Besides, without you, Eli and I never would have lasted. We weren't complete until you came into our lives...and our bed."

Sally smacked him and looked over at Nova and Nola's daughter, Ambrose, who didn't seem to notice the grown up talk as she chatted with her grandmother, Ms. Brown, about her friends at daycare.

"Guys. You're getting ahead of yourselves here." Quinn rolled his eyes. "I've known them for all of a day. Yeah, they're both smoking hot. And yeah, there was definitely some sexy vibes going on, but that's nothing like knowing someone for years and realizing they're your life partner."

"It has to start somewhere," Gavyn said, shocking the hell out of Quinn, who figured the Hot Rides owner would want none of this drama impacting business. "I was there. What I saw today was...kind of magical. You three clicked right away. And I don't think you were the only one noticing the possibilities. Being close-minded and shutting people out when they need you is, in principle, equally as bad as coming between two people who would suffer from your interference."

"If I could do it all over again, I'd never wait so long to act on what every bit of my soul was telling me to do." Eli grimaced. "It's the biggest regret of my life that I didn't take action sooner. Think of all the time I wasted. It makes me sick."

Sally hugged Eli. "We're together now. That's what matters."

"All I'm saying is that both Bryce and Gavyn noticed something special. They've seen you with plenty of your fuck buddies and never mentioned it to me before." Roman bumped his forearm into Quinn's gently. "We want you to be happy and this was the first time they've seen you smile like that in far too long."

"No one's going to be smiling if this goes bad," Quinn grumbled, afraid to hope that the Hot Rods were right. What were the odds that he'd found exactly the two people he'd been searching for since he realized he was bi and that it might take more than one partner to satisfy him?

"You're right, little bro." Roman squeezed Quinn's shoulder. The touch didn't bother him because he trusted his brother to the bone. Roman would never hurt him. And the tender reminder made Quinn pay extra attention to the advice he was about to impart. He only wanted to help. "It's too soon to know anything yet. But sometimes you have to gamble to win. So all we're trying to say is keep your heart open and listen to what it tells you."

"That's some good advice right there." Tom nodded and pointed with his fork. He wrapped his arm around Ms. Brown and pulled her toward him so he could plant a loud smack on her cheek. "We raised some damn fine kids, Willie."

"We have indeed." She angled her face to kiss Tom more deeply on the lips.

Ambrose shrieked, "Ick. Gramma and Gramps. Not at the dinner table."

Quinn cracked up along with the rest of the gang. Then he took a deep breath for the first time since Trevon had dropped the Devra bomb on him. They were right. Things would work out as they should. They always did. But how rough would the road be between here and there?

8

The next few days passed quietly as they settled into their new routines. After Quinn got home from the Hot Rods family dinner, he helped Trevon and Devra make the cottage next door to his livable again. They worked together, moving all the stuff he'd had stored over there to the garage, dusted everything, turned on the water, and made sure the air conditioning was working. He brought over some spare sheets and pillows so they'd have fresh bedding and tried not to think about what they'd be doing on his linens.

He didn't ask where they'd been staying, but it was clear they needed a roof over their heads as much as Trevon had needed the job at Hot Rides.

Devra made no mention of her work situation or how she'd get there from their location on the outskirts of town, so he didn't pry. He figured they'd tell him more about themselves in time, if they felt like it. Honestly, learning details was risky. The danger was he'd like them more and more instead of less and less.

Quinn couldn't afford to grow feelings for either of

them. Lusting after them was bad enough in these close quarters.

He'd spent his evenings trying not to spy on them from his favorite place to sit and read on his back porch. But they were hard to ignore. Their bursts of laughter couldn't be contained in the small space. They often drew his wistful gaze. And when he saw them in the soft glow of the living room lamp as they engaged in late-night discussions on the sofa, it made him wonder what they were talking about.

He wasn't sure if it was a blessing or a curse that he hadn't seen them touching in a non-platonic way. No kissing, no cuddling, no...nothing. Maybe they were more discreet than he was, especially with Trevon's boss so close, but he didn't get the sense that was true.

Sometimes they seemed more like best friends and perfect roommates than the lovers he knew they were. Damn, if they didn't make him envious.

Just like all the other happy couples, or trios, or whatever matchups in his life. He'd spent so long as the odd one out, he might not know what to do if he was ever included inside the bright circle of a relationship himself. Maybe he should get a cat or a dog. Then at least he'd have someone to take care of, and talk to, and pet.

Not the worst idea he'd ever had.

Quinn set down his tools and rested his back up against a support pole nearby as he debated a trip to the animal shelter after work. It was either that or prowl around the bars again tonight, and he couldn't imagine that satisfying his cravings. He glanced over at Trevon, who was in the middle of a tune-up. Quinn would actually get out of here at a reasonable time this evening. But where would he go? What would he do?

No other guy was going to hold the same appeal as the one bent over that engine, his fingers working magic on the shiny metal. His pants were riding low on his waist, exposing the very top edge of his tight ass and the curves that kept them from pooling around his ankles. Not that Quinn would mind if that were to happen.

He dropped his head back, closed his eyes, and willed his partially hard cock to wilt instead of going full erection. It was a constant struggle around Trevon and Devra, who'd taken to hanging out with them during the afternoons after she'd spent a few hours cleaning, working on reviving the cottage's garden, and cooking them some of the most delicious lunches he'd ever had.

Sorry, Ms. Brown.

In fact, his stomach growled then as he smelled spicy, foreign food. When he opened his eyes, Devra was there, holding a tray at least half as big as herself, grinning down at him. "Asleep on the job? Don't worry, I won't tell your worker."

Quinn scrambled to his feet, embarrassed both at being busted daydreaming about their sweet asses and for looking like a slacker. He took the tray from her and carried it to a table in the break room. "Just needed a minute."

"You're the boss. I'm sure you could go take a half-hour nap on your lunch break if you need. Trevon and I can handle stuff here. Gavyn said he'd be around later in case you'd feel better if we were supervised." She looked down at the spread she'd prepared and fiddled with the dishes, straightening things for no reason.

"It's not that I don't trust you two here." Oddly, that was the truth. Though he'd only known them a few days, they already felt like part of the Hot Rides family. Nothing they'd shown him yet had given him even a moment to pause and consider their dependability. "It's more like... Well, honestly, I wouldn't know what to do with myself if it wasn't for Hot Rides and working here."

Right then, the phone rang. Quinn jogged over to the office, on the other side of the wall from the break room, and answered it. He rummaged around Gavyn's desk until he retrieved the appointment book and found an empty slot that worked for the customer who wanted to put fancy new tires on his bike. When he hung up, Devra was watching him thoughtfully.

"You know, you might as well let me help with that stuff," she said as he hung up the phone. "I spend a lot of time hanging out here. I think I can manage to take calls and write down some messages when you're working on a motorcycle so that you don't have to pull double duty."

"That's not necessary." Quinn was happy enough to have Trevon taking half the workload in the shop. It really did leave him some time to relax. Time to realize how much he'd been overdoing it lately.

"It'd be nice to be useful for once." Devra's smile didn't quite make it past her mouth. The sad twist of her burgundy lips made Quinn want to reach out and hug her, except he didn't know what Trevon would think of that. "You've been so generous with us. I'd like to give back in some way if I'm able."

What would it hurt? It wasn't a terrible idea. Amber and her sister, Nola, took care of some administrative stuff when they could, but that wasn't their primary focus.

Quinn made a snap decision. "I'm willing to pay you for your time. No one's asking you to work for free."

"Thank you, but..." Devra glanced over at Trevon, who

didn't appear to be listening to their conversation. "I can't accept that."

"Of course you can." Quinn tried to ignore their weird dynamic. Or at least to treat them as individuals instead of a unit. They were both fascinating to him in their own ways. Devra deserved a shot at least as much as Trevon had. Maybe more now that he'd gotten to know her a bit. She was strong, independent, and yet reserved, as if afraid to overstep.

She'd taken initiative and he'd much rather nurture that than squash it.

"No. Legally, I can't." She shrugged one shoulder. "I'm not a US citizen. I don't even have my green card yet. We haven't been married that long and once I was eligible to apply, we didn't have the money to submit my paperwork. Besides, it can take a while to process..."

Devra sighed. "So yeah, I'm kind of useless. Can't drive, can't work, can't vote. Can't do much of anything. Sometimes I feel like Trevon's child more than his wife, to be honest. We've been struggling and there's nothing I can do about it. I'm just another burden for him, really. I even got turned away as a volunteer for the soup kitchen downtown because of the background check. So I guess you'll have to put up with my cooking instead."

"I love your food." Quinn reached out and took her hand. He held it for far too brief a moment, caressing her soft, warm skin before letting it go. He should bite his tongue, but instead he said, "I didn't realize. Sorry. So where are you from?"

He had to know where she'd gotten that seductive accent that lent a bit of a roll to her R's. It drove him wild, and made her seem even more different than the

Midwestern women he'd known before. To him, that was a plus.

"Yemen." She rocked back when she said it, almost as if the memory of her home made her flinch. "It's a beautiful country, but it's not...safe...for me right now. My father sent me here with a one-way plane ticket."

"So you're a refugee." Quinn paused, setting the appointment book down next to the tray of dishes she'd lovingly prepared for Trevon...and for him.

He wasn't the greatest at geography, but he knew she was from somewhere in the Middle East. That explained her gorgeous skin and dark, wavy hair. In a flash, he imagined her wearing more traditional clothing, her eyes outlined heavily, and her hair peeking out from beneath a lace head wrap. He cleared his throat as he pictured how stunning she would be in her native environment and how beautifully she'd adapted to his. He admired her flexibility and the courage it must have taken to adjust to an entirely new world under difficult circumstances.

Devra wrung her hands as if she was as nervous talking to him about this as he was about prying or learning something that might take his admiration to someplace deeper. Someplace strictly off limits. "I was supposed to go to college here. But my father disappeared and so did the funds in our bank account. I heard from one of my cousins that...he was killed along with most everyone else in our town who spoke up against the injustices that are being committed there."

"Jesus, Devra. I'm so sorry. That's...sick." Quinn reined in his outrage and disgust lest she think it was aimed at her and a situation out of her control. But he couldn't help it—he hugged her although he knew too well it wouldn't do much to soothe the hurt.

"It is." Her voice was monotone, as if she had accepted it by now, or maybe as if she was still in shock and numb to the horror of it all. "I had to drop out. I lost my work-study position at...um...the place where I met Trevon. I was stranded. Utterly alone. He took me in and made us family. I owe Trevon everything. He saved my life."

"I'm sure he would do it a million times over for the woman he loves." Quinn knew he sure as hell would. No one deserved to live in fear like that. No one deserved to be cast aside instead of being welcomed with open arms.

Devra winced and turned away. The heavy conversation must have been too much for her.

Just then, the phone rang again. She lunged for it without asking this time. Quinn wouldn't have had the heart to tell her not to anyway. Not after what she'd shared. He'd felt useless once, too, until his brother and Hot Rods—then Hot Rides—had given him a purpose.

Her voice was loud and clear when she said, "Hot Rides Garage. How can I help you?"

Trevon whipped his gaze to Devra. Then to Quinn, who shrugged.

He understood what it was like to rely on the kindness of strangers. Hell, he'd been all alone, thrust into a foreign setting, after his brother had rescued him from their mother's home and the abuse he'd suffered at her hands. It paled in comparison to Devra's situation, but he had a taste of what she must have experienced. If he hadn't been allowed to chip in at Hot Rods, he probably would have gone crazy or run away before they'd become family in the truest sense of the word. He had no desire to be a pity case. A proud woman like her would feel the same.

If answering a dumb phone call was what it took to

make Devra feel like she belonged and had some worth, who the fuck was he to tell her not to do it?

"Yes, sir. Wednesday at 3PM would be fine. We'll see you then." Devra jotted down a note in the planner, then hung up the phone.

Her smile nearly blinded Quinn. Straight, white teeth stood out against her rouged mouth and the color infusing her cheeks for the first time since he'd met her. So he figured he'd do one better and show her how much he enjoyed her meals as well.

"Trevon, you better get your ass in here for lunch before I eat yours, too." Quinn froze when Devra covered her mouth with her hand. She looked away, blushing.

Well, he hadn't meant it like that, but... Yeah, that, too.

"One minute, I'm cleaning up." Trevon hustled, joining them in less than half that time.

Meanwhile, Quinn had already heaped his plate with a helping of each dish Devra had whipped up. "So, what is it I'm eating here? I like this orange stuff you made yesterday, too."

Devra laughed, making Trevon pause. He grinned at her, then flashed Quinn a grateful smile. Apparently he liked it when Quinn made his wife happy. Good. Because Quinn thought it might be his new favorite pastime.

As he stuffed his face, Devra told him the names of each food and its ingredients. Hummus, shafoot, falafel, and lamb mandi. He was stuffed by the time he'd eaten half of what he'd taken. That didn't stop him from finishing every last bit and licking his fingers at the end.

He looked up to find both Devra and Trevon staring at him. "What?"

Hell, he hadn't even belched.

Trevon cleared his throat and shook his head. Devra beamed. She asked, "You liked it that much?"

"Uh huh." He grinned a little self-consciously.

"Trevon tells me it's good, but I thought he might be just being nice. That's how he is." Devra smiled shyly. "I was studying to be a chef and taking business classes before...you know."

Trevon put his hand on her knee and squeezed.

"My dream was that someday I could open a restaurant with a traditional menu so I could introduce more people to our food." She sighed and shook herself, then stood to clear the dishes.

"Wait...why *was*?" Quinn asked.

"We're so far from making that possible. For now, we need to concentrate on getting by." Devra reached out and took his dirty plate and crumpled napkin. "Because of you, we're in a much better place than we were a week ago. I can imagine, someday, things could be different than they have been lately. So thank you, Quinn. Thank you."

Trevon didn't object when his wife circled the table and smothered Quinn in a hug.

It startled him so much that he wasn't sure if he should hug her back or pretend like her embrace hadn't touched him so much deeper than his chest and back. He felt her energy radiate straight to his soul. For the first time in forever, it felt like he was doing something right.

Like he was where he was supposed to be and doing shit that really mattered.

They might not know it, but Trevon and Devra were as good for him as he was for them.

He made a mental note to pick up a bunch of seeds on his next trip to the hardware store. Things that Devra had listed as her main ingredients—zucchini, garlic, eggplant, and tomatoes—to start. It was the least he could do if he planned to eat her food every chance he got.

Plus, it would be interesting to see what they could grow together.

9

"That was my last appointment for the day." Quinn sank to the floor next to where Trevon was cleaning his tools. Though Trevon tried not to stare, he couldn't help taking a quick scan and absorbing every detail about Quinn. The guy rested his back against the metal cabinets and draped his tattooed arms over his bent knees while he kept his boots planted on the concrete. His muscles were casually on display. He was the very definition of masculinity.

"I'm finished, too." It was just the two of them holding down the garage. Since Trevon had come on board, Gavyn had been taking the opportunity to travel to conventions where they could rack up some more work from collectors and enthusiasts.

Stuff more interesting than routine maintenance. Knowing they had more varied and specialized work coming in was exciting for Trevon, too. Working here would definitely boost his resume.

"You know my friends are probably grilling your poor wife right now." Quinn picked at his jeans. Though he said it casually, Trevon could tell he was kind of worried. About what?

Devra had gone with some of the Hot Rods ladies to get a manicure or a massage or some other spa shit. Whatever girls did at those fancy places. Devra had originally turned down their offer, since they didn't have the cash for those kind of luxuries, but the women had refused to take no for an answer. A gorgeous, no-nonsense lady named Sally had rolled up in a neon-pink convertible classic Mustang and convinced Devra by explaining they were getting freebies in exchange for reviews of a new establishment.

Quinn had let it slip later that Sally had fudged the truth a bit. He'd promised that the women were happy to chip in so that Devra could join them, especially since they were truly getting a hefty discount for being guinea pigs. Trevon would ordinarily have objected, except Devra deserved to be pampered. If he couldn't do it for her, he would accept help to provide the things she needed. Ego be damned.

"She can hold her own." Trevon grinned, thinking of his petite yet fierce wife. "She might be soft spoken, but she's tough. Besides, it would be awesome for her to have her own friends to hang out with instead of being stuck with me all the damn time. I'm not always the best company."

"I don't know. I've enjoyed my time at the shop a lot more since you arrived. Having someone to talk to makes the days go by a lot faster." Quinn didn't look at Trevon when he admitted it.

The declaration alone made Trevon's heart race and his palms sweat. He was in serious trouble. The more time he spent with Quinn, the more he realized that the guy was every bit as generous, compassionate, and sexy as he'd first appeared.

"You're a hell of a lot better to deal with than Vance," Trevon managed.

Quinn cracked up at that. "God, I hope so. That guy is such a dick."

Trevon shrugged. "I don't blame him for giving me the boot. Anyway, it turned out for the best."

He had finished wiping grease from his fingers and was mid-stretch when he noticed Quinn staring at the flexing muscles of his chest and abdomen. Maybe he should have kept his shirt on despite the heat of the waxing summer. Or maybe that odd look on his face had something to do with what he was about to say and not Trevon's body being on display.

"Why don't you go get your bike and bring it in here? I've been thinking...if you want, we could tinker around with it when it's slow or after hours," Quinn suggested. The way he said it made Trevon sure it wasn't as offhanded a comment as he'd like Trevon to think.

"First, is it ever slow here?" Trevon wondered. Truth was, there was enough work for two additional mechanics and they turned down nearly as much business as they could accept. The waitlist for even routine maintenance stretched out for weeks.

Gavyn was throwing money away by not staffing this place appropriately. There was plenty of room for more workstations. So why were they so shorthanded?

"Not lately." Quinn puffed up. "Hot Rides is gaining a reputation good enough that people bring their motorcycles from up to two states away for us to modify them. Between you and me, I think Gavyn has been a little hesitant to expand because he's afraid of the pressure.

When we were a small shop, it was easy to manage and success was guaranteed. Taking on more means risking more. And for him that's a lot to handle..."

Quinn scrubbed his hand over his mouth as if he was debating revealing more.

"What?" Trevon was curious sure, but he felt like maybe he could help them. And the thought of being useful instead of a problem for once...well, that was damn attractive.

"Gavyn's a recovering alcoholic. Stress could be a trigger for him falling into bad habits. He knows it and so do we." Quinn met Trevon's gaze then, as if daring him to think badly of the shop's owner. If anything, though, it raised his esteem. To know that Gavyn had overcome his struggles...it was damn impressive. Maybe someday Trevon would be able to say the same. Although his issues didn't stem from substance abuse, they often seemed insurmountable. All they could do, any of them, was try their best.

"I know. He told me when I asked him to share a beer with me on the deck the other night." Trevon admitted to himself that he'd been hurt by the guy's emphatic rejection until he'd explained why he'd declined. It had also made Trevon feel like less of an outcast to know that even these men, whom he looked up to already, had problems. Life wasn't easy for any of them. If they could overcome some pretty steep hurdles, so could he.

"Oh. Yep." Quinn smiled wryly. "Don't take this personally, but I'm so glad he did. It's been a while now, maybe five years, even still..."

"I won't make that mistake again. In fact, I won't bring anymore booze to the house." Trevon didn't mind. He'd really only bought that six pack in the hopes of bonding with the other guys.

"Probably for the best. My brother, Roman, and Gavyn met in rehab. I don't drink at all, since I've got shit genes for it. Saw what it did to Roman and my mom. That was plenty for me. Anyway, I think for a while Gavyn was making sure he had everything under control, you know? The fact that he's willing to take these next steps now makes me really happy and nervous, too. You showed up at the perfect time."

"You have no idea." Trevon released a deep breath. Each day that he worked at Hot Rides and nothing imploded, he relaxed some. He was still amped up enough to realize how close he'd been to his limit when he'd met Quinn. Hearing more about these guys and learning they had their own vulnerabilities made him more willing to share his own. "That tent and the ratty sleeping bags we have aren't only for fun. It's not so bad this time of year, but last winter sucked. I don't want Devra to have to go through that again. Ever."

"Shit, Trevon. That's fucking rough." Quinn looked as if he might reach out. Instead, he cleared his throat then said, "I'm glad Hot Rides is able to be a place for you like Hot Rods was for me. A safe haven and an answer to a lot of prayers I didn't think anyone was listening to."

What could Quinn have needed saving from? He was an absolute badass who lived a privileged life with a support network that made Trevon and Devra seem like they were stranded on a desert island surrounded by a sea of despair in comparison.

"So what do you think?" Quinn steered them away from dangerous, emotional territory. "Should we work on your bike?"

"Are you asking because it would be entertaining for you to have a side project or because you think I need another helping hand?" Okay, both were probably true. Still, there was only so much pity Trevon could stand before his pride rebelled.

"I don't have much of a social life. Humor me. Let's do something fun. Put our skills to good use and fix up your motorcycle." Quinn paused. "If it was fully restored, it would be worth a crap load of money. Between that and your job here, you'd be good."

Trevon froze at that. "I'm not sure it would ever be worth more to someone else than me. It's the last piece of my family and my legacy I have left. I've lost...everything else."

"So is that where you got it? You inherited it? I've been wondering." Quinn leaned forward, eager to hear more.

"Yeah. Pop—that's my grandfather—brought it back with him after the war. No idea how he managed that. It sat in his barn for decades after he got too unsteady to ride it. Over time, he couldn't keep up with the maintenance. Not that it was in pristine condition even then. He never saw it as a showpiece, but as a practical vehicle. Later in life, I think it was a reminder of his younger days. I took care of him the past few years. Tried to keep up with his farm, his health, and a million other things, including the bike. It got to be too much. He had a series of small strokes. Then dementia set in. After that, he got prostate cancer. He needed full-time care from actual nurses who knew what they were doing. It cost a fortune. But even when he didn't know who I was anymore, he would still tell me stories about that motorcycle and the places it had taken him."

Quinn got up and wandered closer as Trevon was

talking. He thought for one crazy moment that Quinn might open his strong arms and hold him until the terrible dread eased out of his gut. But Trevon couldn't let that happen. Because it wouldn't stop there.

The spark of attraction that had flared between them from the first moment hadn't been snuffed out over time. Instead, it had built into an inferno. One he couldn't run away from or put out. It was too mesmerizing and warmed him simply from being near it.

So he closed his eyes and turned away.

"It sounds like you did everything you could for him." Quinn put his hand on Trevon's shoulder instead. Even that was enough to send a jolt of awareness straight down his spine to his cock.

It had been so fucking long...

"I tried my best." Trevon shrugged, dislodging Quinn's fingers.

"You're a good person," Quinn said softly. "I may not have known you for long, but I see how you look out for Devra. You always put her first. Even when she told you to test the hammock after your shift the other day, you were out there mowing your damn lawn and mine, too. I saw those flowers you dug up out of the woods and planted along the walkway for her yesterday."

They were caring and respectful to each other. That wasn't a problem.

Trevon wondered if Quinn had noticed yet that they never went beyond politeness to true intimacy. Maybe he assumed Devra was shy or that her upbringing made public displays of affection uncomfortable for her.

It might have been Trevon's imagination, but he thought he saw Quinn eyeing Devra as often as he was leveling those smoldering gazes in Trevon's direction.

He didn't blame the guy. Devra was gorgeous. Any man would want her. He sure as shit did. Trevon was married to her and yet he could never truly have her. "Those little things don't make up for...everything else."

"The stuff she talked about yesterday didn't sound so inconsequential to me." Quinn's voice was sterner. "You heard what she said. You saved her life."

"Just because she's alive doesn't mean she's living well." Trevon rubbed his gut and the familiar ache there. "She didn't tell you the whole story. In fact, she left out some pretty important and damning shit. To make me look better."

Quinn tried again. "Or maybe she doesn't see things the same way you do."

He was relentless. Unfortunately, he was also wrong.

So Trevon laid it out. He disclosed the cold, hard facts that made him look like the leech he was. "Her father sent her here for an education. For a better life. My grandfather had some distant connection to her dad through a friend of a military friend. They'd never even met or spoken before he reached out. My grandfather was already ill. Racking up tons of medical bills. Her dad was loaded. A successful businessman in their country. He agreed to pay off our debt if we'd watch over Devra. She'd been sheltered and now she was here, in a land full of temptations and pitfalls, on her own. He essentially bought us to protect her."

"I'd say he chose well since you two fell in love, got married, and have been battling life's bullshit side-by-side," Quinn said, proving he still didn't get it.

Not at all.

Devra hadn't picked Trevon. She'd been stuck with him. He was a necessary evil, not a man she considered her soul mate. And that's why he'd never make an advance on her. Not a single kiss, and certainly not anything more.

Because Devra didn't have a choice.

What would it make him if he took her up on the coy glances she sometimes gave him or the time she'd offered, on their wedding night, to lie down for him?

The thought made him sick.

"Yeah, well..." He'd try one more time to explain. "Of course, we'd have looked after Devra anyway, for free, but my grandfather was worried about me. We'd already sold everything except a small guesthouse on his farm and..."

"His motorcycle." Quinn winced.

"That bike is all I have left of him and the rest of my family." Trevon's shoulders slumped. "I'm not sure I can give it up for any amount of money."

Could he be more selfish and weak?

In that moment, Trevon loathed himself even more than usual.

10

"Hey, Devra is your family now. So am I. Hot Rides, and Hot Rods, are your place, too. If that's what you want. We're a collection of misfits and vagabonds, really. You'll fit right in." Quinn had already thought Trevon was perfect for the shop. Now he knew it to his core. The guy was one of them whether he realized it yet or not.

"Thanks, but I'm not sure I belong." Trevon backed up a step and then another. "See, my grandfather took that money from Devra's dad. He paid off our debts and put the rest in a trust for his care so we'd never have to worry about it again. What he didn't know was that Devra's father would be killed. That their family's wealth would disappear overnight along with her dad's body. And that Devra wouldn't have enough money to finish her schooling so she could land a job that came with a legit visa."

Quinn was really hoping this wasn't going where he thought it might be headed.

"For that matter, we haven't even had enough cash to

pay for a green card for her. Well, technically we had about a thousand bucks reserved for it, but I fucked up the paperwork. There are a ton of rules and it's confusing as hell. I did something wrong. So we have to fix it and reapply. Now we need at least twice or maybe three times as much money so we can hire an immigration lawyer to sort the stuff I jacked up and then restart the process, which could take pretty much forever anyway. Devra has very little freedom. We've struggled. She hasn't been much better off here than she would have been back home."

"That's absurd, Trevon. Her father is dead. Anything's better than that. Plus, she has you. A partner, a confidant, a lover, and a soul mate. To me, those are the most valuable things in life." Quinn would give anything to have those. If he were matched up, like all his other friends and relatives, he could power through anything else. Why didn't Trevon see that?

The guy opened his mouth, then shut it. He opened it again with a growl of frustration, then barked, "It's not like that, okay?"

"What? What do you mean?" Quinn grew still and quiet. He waited for Trevon to get a grip on the despair wrinkling his usually smooth features.

"Here's the truth." Trevon smacked his palm on the scuffed bench top, making Quinn wince. "We're essentially roommates. She agreed to marry me so that I could live up to my promise to protect her. Keep her here. I've never made love to Devra. In fact, I've never even kissed her. You know, like an on-the-mouth, kiss-me-until-we're-naked kiss. In fact, I'm pretty sure my wife is a virgin."

Quinn's jaw dropped. He sputtered for a few moments

until he could say, "You're a motherfucking saint, you know that? How can you possibly resist that much temptation? Forget Gavyn and that beer you offered him. Devra is..."

"Gorgeous, sweet, resilient, funny, kind, a great cook..." Trevon groaned. "Yeah, I know."

"What the hell are you waiting for? Go pick some of those flowers, light a couple friggin' candles, and seduce the hell out of her when she comes home!" Quinn was gesturing like an old lady who'd gotten riled up by neighborhood hooligans toilet-papering her house. His hands flailed as his eyes bugged out.

It might have been funny if they weren't discussing something so painful to Trevon, who seemed to deflate in front of his eyes. "Stop, Quinn. I can't."

"Why not?" Quinn nearly shouted. "Because if I was you, I'd be all over that."

"I want her." Trevon frowned. "Desperately. I can't have her. It's not right."

"You're *married*. By just about any standards in the world, including the ones in Devra's country, I'm pretty sure, you are good to go." Quinn leaned in. "What's the problem?"

He could think of one major possibility that had to do with the way Trevon was staring at his mouth, even now.

"It has to be her choice. I mean, a real decision." Trevon shrugged. "And I can never guarantee that's the case. We're married. She'll feel obligated. In fact, she offered once on our wedding night. I turned her away. You're right. That's how she was raised, to obey her husband. And I don't want sex with me to be another duty for her. The cost of her freedom."

75

Quinn was speechless. "A *duty*? I'd gladly fuck you any day of the week."

Trevon didn't say a word. He didn't even blink. Quinn thought he might not even be breathing anymore.

"Oh shit. I shouldn't have said that." Quinn tugged on his hair and started to ramble in the hopes that something he said would keep Trevon from running away. Or worse, from grabbing Devra and driving both of them out of his life for good. He'd only just found them. The thought of them going was...frightening and he couldn't quite say why. "Sorry. Ignore me. And...maybe you're right. It was easy to say that because I don't *have* to fuck you. I mean, not that anyone's fucking anyone but in theory, I get your point."

Trevon was still staring. Not blinking. Totally in shock.

For endless moments, they stood there looking at each other. Thinking. Processing. Not speaking. Not moving. And definitely not touching. Trying to figure a way out of the mess he'd put them in.

Eventually Quinn cleared his throat. "I'm sorry. I got carried away. Here's what I should have said: Devra's here. She's alive. And as long as you two keep fighting for a better future, you can untangle the rest as you go."

Both of them pretended like all the rest—especially the part about fucking—had never come out of his mouth. Quinn wished he had never dropped those bombs. Yet, he couldn't stop himself from wanting to drop a few more.

"I would argue with you, but this week has been a massive turnaround." Trevon did crack a smile then. "I keep thinking I'm dreaming, to be honest. You have no idea how much you've done for us."

The two men looked at each other, weighing the person in front of them.

"I think I'm starting to understand." Quinn scrunched his eyes closed. "Can I ask one more stupid question before we act like this conversation never happened?"

"Just one. I think that's all I can take." Trevon clutched his chest though the corner of his mouth quirked up in a self-deprecating smile.

Quinn blurted his query before he could tell himself it was a dumb idea to ask. "Does Devra know you're into men?"

Was that part of the reason Trevon was holding back? Maybe he wasn't bi, but gay. Maybe no matter the circumstances, he'd never be intimate with Devra because physical intimacy with a woman simply wasn't his thing.

If that was the case, Quinn got it. He just thought it would be kinder for Trevon to be honest, with himself and his wife, so that they didn't have to abstain from one of life's greatest pleasures. They could have a nontraditional arrangement. Maybe one where they were life partners who slept with other people. It wouldn't be the weirdest thing Quinn had ever heard of. Look at the Powertools crew and the Hot Rods. They'd created their own idyllic situations, even if it broke a lot of the rules most of society upheld in relationships.

In Quinn's world, anything was okay so long as everyone involved was honest, up front, and in agreement. Maybe selfishly he was trying to figure out a way, even now, that he could have one half—or both halves—of his new favorite couple for himself.

Clearly he wasn't nearly as good a man as Trevon was when it came to integrity.

"No. She doesn't." Trevon pinched the bridge of his

nose. "I'm afraid to tell her. I don't know what her beliefs about it are given her culture."

"It's never come up?" Quinn called bullshit. "Come on."

"I guess I've avoided the topic as best I can." Trevon shrugged. "It's bad enough to know that she's not in love with me. It would kill me if she looked at me with disgust."

"So you haven't slept with anyone in how long?" Quinn should really shut up now.

"Two years or so." Trevon groaned. "I would never cheat on her."

That word, *cheat*, hit Quinn hard. That was a line he swore he'd never cross. Too bad he hadn't considered all the possible circumstances that might lead him to sleeping with a married person. He wasn't sure what the right answer was in a situation this...gray.

He knew what his dick thought about it, though. It wanted to end Trevon's dry spell, and Devra's, too. That didn't mean he'd give in to his wicked fantasies.

Then Trevon continued, "And even then...I never... with a guy, I mean. I wanted to, but it just never happened. Never found the right person. We lived in the middle of nowhere and I was taking care of Pop by the time I was seventeen."

Attempting to be a better person than he felt like at the moment, Quinn swore to himself that he'd be there for his new friend as the guy warred with himself over the best way to honor the vows he'd taken, and obviously had meant. No matter how desperately he wanted to be the right person Trevon had been looking for. "You haven't had much freedom either, Trevon. Maybe you need to talk to Devra about that, for both your sakes. You might be surprised by her reaction."

"You know what? I think you're right." Trevon shocked Quinn.

Was he reconsidering a physical relationship, either with his wife or with Quinn? Would Quinn have the willpower to do what was right if Trevon reached for him right then?

"About Devra?" he asked.

"No." Trevon huffed. "About the bike. We should fix it up and see if anyone wants her. If that's what it takes to hire a lawyer to figure out all those fucking rules, pay for Devra's green card application, and get her back on track with school, we should do it. If we get lucky and there's even some left to put a down payment on a building for the restaurant she's dreaming about, there's no question in my mind. Because only then, when she's able to stand on her own, will I know for sure if she's choosing to stay with me or if she would rather be free if she could be."

Quinn hesitated now that he knew what the motorcycle meant to Trevon. He didn't want the guy to lose the last tie he had to his heritage and memories of better days. "Maybe you were right. To you, it's priceless..."

"Devra's worth it. Every bit of elbow grease and every penny we might raise. Let's do this. Let's bring the bike back to life. If nothing else, my pop would have approved of that. It's going to take a while, so we might as well do what we can as we can. What happens after that remains to be seen, but at least I'll have options. *Devra* will have options." Trevon nodded to himself as if reconfirming his line of thinking.

Then he stepped closer, surprising Quinn when he

flung a single arm around his shoulder and smacked it twice in a quick bro-hug. Even that was enough to spread flames of desire to every cell of Quinn's body.

He leaned in to Trevon's embrace. And when he looked up at the other guy, whose eyes were glassy and wide, Quinn thought about how easy it would be to tip his face a fraction of an inch and seal their lips together.

For a moment, they hung there on the precipice of something thrilling and dangerous. Then Trevon stumbled backward, wiping his hands on his jeans. Were they as sweaty as Quinn's? "Give me a couple minutes."

"Yeah. I could use them, too." Quinn was breathing hard.

"When I come back, can we forget we had this discussion?" Trevon wondered.

Quinn would always remember. Not for an instant could he blank out Trevon's determination and the sacrifices he'd made to care for his family, including Devra. Neither would he get over Devra's bravery or her resilience.

These two were fighters. They were exceptional. They were people he wanted in his life.

So Quinn nodded and lied, "Yeah. We can do that. Go ahead. Go get the bike."

Without a backward glance, Trevon marched out of the garage toward the cottage where he'd left the 1938 Indian Chief that could be the key to unlocking his destiny before Quinn could attempt to change his mind.

He wasn't sure if he was thrilled or pissed off at himself for putting the idea in Trevon's mind. It did, however, prove to him that once he opened his mouth, he couldn't always take back what he said. He'd have to be more careful from then on.

Especially when it came to Trevon and Devra's relationship.

No matter how badly he wanted to repair them, he might have to settle for watching and supporting them as they tried to fix themselves.

Quinn spun away, practically dashing into the break room. He shut the door, slammed his back up against the cold metal, and breathed hard, staring at the ceiling. When even that wasn't cooling him down, he crossed to the refrigerator and stuck his head in the freezer until his ears were in danger of frostbite.

It was going to be a long, hot summer.

11

Devra moaned as the masseuse worked out kinks in her neck and shoulders that had been there so long, she'd forgotten what it felt like when the muscles unknotted. Hell, she probably had just gotten two inches taller. The woman's healing hands drifted lower over Devra's buttocks and the backs of her thighs, turning her into a tingling blob of serenity. If she wasn't careful, she might fall asleep soon.

Sally's friend Kayla, who was married to one of the hunky construction workers the ladies had told her all about, was an expert massage therapist. She'd apparently been mentoring the woman who owned this spa, and the Hot Rods women were doing their part to help her build her clientele by indulging in world class treatments in exchange for some honest reviews on the company's website.

Devra hoped *"bone-meltingly good"* sufficed, because it was true.

As soon as she had stepped inside the retreat, which felt like an oasis nestled amidst the chaos of the outside world, she'd began to relax. Worries and fears that usually plagued her receded. With her mind clear and her body unwound, she felt her lips loosening, too.

It was easy to chat with the Hot Rods ladies about their jobs, their kids, and especially their relationships. Okay, so far she'd mostly observed and giggled at their antics, wondering what it would be like to have a circle of female friends that close around her.

Still, it was nearly as refreshing as the spa treatments they were enjoying together.

Their easy banter and teasing helped Devra overcome some of her nerves, too. Though she'd been in this country for nearly two years now, she didn't always feel as comfortable being as free with her thoughts, emotions—and definitely not with her body—as women who'd grown up here generally seemed to be. Customs in her homeland were as dissimilar from those here as the food people ate in each place. Though she embraced the differences, she was still easily scandalized in new situations even if she tried not to show it.

That was one of the reasons she hadn't been more aggressive with Trevon.

This time her groan was not one of pleasure. *Damn it.*

Devra desperately clung to the tranquility around her. She needed a few more moments of peace before she allowed her problems to surface again.

"Are you okay?" The masseuse paused.

"Yes, sorry." Devra adjusted the towel draped over her behind, making sure everything critical was still covered. "My mind was wandering and it went somewhere I wish it hadn't."

"Sounds like boy trouble to me," Sabra muttered from the table beside Devra.

"When is it *not* boy trouble that causes the most grief?" Kaelyn snorted. "Remind me why they're worth it again?"

"Orgasms," Sally announced without hesitation. "Alllllllll the orgasms they give us. That's why they're worth it."

Devra's eyes widened despite the fact that her face was buried in a soft towel. Had Sally really said that out loud in public? Without thinking, she said, "I'm plenty capable of achieving those on my own."

The women, including the masseuse, cracked up at that.

"True. But it's so much more fun with them," Nola practically purred.

Devra wouldn't know. She'd never been intimate with a man. Not even her own husband. She was careful to keep that fact to herself. These women would never understand. And the factoid would not only ostracize her, but it could also endanger her if someone was to get the wrong idea and report her to Immigration. Everything she and Trevon had struggled for could be for nothing.

The room lights gradually increased as their massage session ended. Devra heard rustling around her and tipped her head. Squinting, she realized the other women were sitting up, so she did too, careful to hug her towel over her otherwise exposed skin.

She swayed slightly on the table, amazed at how different she felt.

"Looks like you really needed that," Sally said with a soft laugh that wasn't unkind.

"More than I realized." Devra sighed and tipped her neck from side to side, thrilled to find it didn't ache anymore. "Wow."

"Maybe I need to have a talk with that studly husband of yours," Nola teased, but the possibility that they'd assume Trevon was to blame only served to introduce some of the tension back into Devra's muscles.

She choked.

"Shit, sorry." Kaelyn smacked Nola's thigh, then reassured Devra, "She's only joking. What happens during girl trips stays at girl trips. We cross our hearts."

"Oh. Right." Devra smiled, but it felt wan even to her.

"I hope you don't mind me saying, though, that Trevon is mighty fine." Sabra added and the other Hot Rods ladies nodded in appreciation.

"I don't. Mind, I mean. It's true." Devra's smile brightened some. "I'm the luckiest woman alive. He takes such good care of me."

Trevon was sinfully sexy. He was so damn tall and strong, he made her feel like no one could ever hurt her. There had never been anyone who came close to him. At least until he'd introduced her to Quinn.

Now they were probably pretty even in her opinion. Some of that, of course, had to do with how they were such good men in addition to how enticing they were. Both of them were decent, honorable, and—yes—very attractive.

"So why isn't he releasing your...tension," Nola wondered. Her sister, Amber—Gavyn's wife—elbowed her in the ribs.

Was it that obvious? Crap.

The other woman hissed, "Not our business."

"Sorry." Nola held her hands up. "I'm not trying to be nosy. Around here don't have many secrets from each other."

Since they'd opened the door a crack, Devra figured

she might do a little digging of her own. "You do seem to be very close. I envy that."

"You can't live together and survive without being blunt and very honest about...well, pretty much everything." Kaelyn spread her hands out in front of her, palms up, as if she was an open book.

"So you all live above the Hot Rods garage then?" Devra had heard them talking about their home but wasn't sure if she had it straight."

"Yep. Everyone except for me and Gavyn. Obviously, since you've seen our house at Hot Rides," Amber confirmed. "We're the boring ones in the bunch."

"So maybe now you see why I needed that damn massage." Sally chuckled, her eyes sparkling. "I mean, with only one man to handle, you should have half the aches and pains!"

"Are you saying...?" Devra didn't dare suggest what she was thinking in case she was wrong. It seemed impossible.

"Oh. Quinn didn't tell you?" Sally shrugged. "Oops. Yup. I have two husbands."

"Is that legal?" Devra asked. Had she misunderstood the law?

"Technically, no," Kaelyn explained. "We have nontraditional relationships. Sally is in love with Eli and Alanso. She is their partner and they're each other's. They love each other equally."

Mind. Blown. Devra sat up straighter. "Is that common here? Have I been missing something? Why didn't anyone tell me?"

Nola laughed. "No, it's unusual, but we do what we like. And we like sharing. A lot."

"Sharing what, exactly?" Devra wondered. Their living

space, obviously. She was getting the feeling there was more she didn't know about them yet.

Kaelyn was the most logical, so she stepped in to help. "I guess in order to fully understand, we need to back up some. Tom, Eli's dad, lost his wife to cancer when Eli was young. Before she got sick, she ran the youth crisis center down the street. And after...Tom took over her mission. He provided a safe place for a lot of kids with troubled pasts, several of whom really bonded with Eli. Alanso, Sally, Kaige, Bryce, Holden, Carver, and Quinn's older brother, Roman. They started the Hot Rods garage together. Over time, their friendship turned into something...more."

Devra thought that sounded incredible. As someone who'd lost her own family and had to start again, she could only imagine how unbreakable bonds like that would become over time and the love you would have for people who'd gone through those things with you. Like Trevon had with her.

"What she's trying to politely say," Sally interjected, "is that I'm in love with Alanso and Eli, and the rest of the guys have paired up with these other lucky ladies, but... sometimes...we like to put on shows for each other or get involved in group sex stuff together. It brings us more pleasure than being with only our partners and— speaking for myself—it makes me feel secure. Like I'll never be alone again."

A tear escaped the corner of Devra's eye before she even realized how deeply what they were saying impacted her. It sounded like heaven.

"Are you okay?" Sabra asked quietly.

Devra nodded.

"Would it be okay if I gave you a hug?" Sally wondered.

Devra nodded again, enthusiastically. It had been so long since she'd experienced physical comfort. Not since she'd left home, really, because Trevon always shied away from her advances. She'd eventually given up trying, realizing her attempts only made him uncomfortable.

Sally damn near crushed her in a bear hug and the rest of the Hot Rods ladies piled on. "Is everything okay?"

"Better than they've been in forever." Devra sniffed and someone handed her a tissue. "Our lives are so different this week from last. I'm grateful. For Quinn and luck or fate or whatever it was that crossed our paths. A week ago, imagining myself being pampered at a spa with a group of ladies like you..."

"Dirty ladies?" Sabra asked with a wink.

"No, genuine, kind, inclusive ones, who've overcome shitty circumstances to find and nurture love in their lives." Devra sighed. "I want you to know how appreciative I am that you brought me with you today and that you're so accepting of me. Of us. I want to be more like you."

"Careful what you wish for!" Nola snorted. "But seriously, I'm glad what we told you didn't scare you away. We weren't sure what your beliefs are..."

Devra shrugged. "Maybe at one time I would have freaked out. Now I'm more open-minded. I've lived through too much to judge other people for finding happiness however they can. I'm still trying to do that."

"Do you have any questions?" Kaelyn asked.

"Tons." Devra nodded again.

"Go ahead. Ask whatever you want. We'll tell you anything you're interested in. Probably more than you can handle." Sabra chuckled as she stretched. The woman was so damn flexible it seemed like she could bend herself in half when she did that.

"How did you figure this out?" Devra couldn't even manage to navigate her relationship with one man successfully, never mind multiple couples and the intricate ties that would come from such an elaborate set up. "And how did you take action on your feelings?"

"Honestly, we waited forever on that part." Sally shook her head. "Eli especially was so afraid that we'd wreck our friendships that he squashed anything extra that started to bubble up. It caused some damage. Almost too much to get over."

"What we've realized since then," Nola added, "is that it's a lot better for everyone if you say what you're feeling when you're feeling it and deal with the repercussions as they come. If you let something build up, it can become too hard to overcome that habitual dusting it under the rug. It seems scarier than it is."

Devra could relate. Now that their immediate crises of where to find shelter and how they'd afford their next meal had passed, she was going to have to talk to Trevon. The thought alone had her shoulders tightening up again.

"Remember that you've got support. You can't get rid of us," Kaelyn promised. "You can talk to us about anything and we won't tattle to your guys. We've got your back."

She cleared her throat, willing to test that theory. "Okay, so... Here's the thing. I'm terrified that Trevon is gay and only married to me because he felt obligated given my situation. What if I'm keeping him from finding love or living a fulfilled life?"

The women simply stared, wide-eyed and open-mouthed for a few seconds.

Devra figured she'd gone far enough that she might as well take their advice and be honest. Once she'd started it felt too good to stop pouring out her anxieties, like draining poison from a wound. "We've never... *I've* never with anyone, so I don't even know what I'm doing. Plus, I think he's attracted to Quinn. And now that he's found someone he would otherwise have pursued if he wasn't stuck with me, I'm scared that things are going to go downhill between us. I have no idea what to do. He's my best friend. I love him. Oh, and, I can totally see why he's into Quinn. Because...I think I am too."

She didn't realize she'd started chewing her thumbnail until Sally put her hand over Devra's and lowered it before saying, "There won't be anything left of your manicure if you do that."

Sabra whistled. "Okay, that's a lot to deal with. No wonder you nearly jumped off the table when the masseuse started in on you. Girl, you have some thinking to do. And then you've got to do something about this or you're going to regret it for the rest of your life."

"I'm sorry to say I think you're right to be afraid." Nola took Devra's hand and squeezed it. "If you stay on this road, you're going to fall apart. You have some hard shit to do if you want to turn this around before it's too late."

"But if you can manage it, everything will be worth it in the end." Sally looked her dead in the eye. "I'm telling you. Your life could be...incredible. All around. Including in bed. Imagine what it would be like if you had both Trevon and Quinn to keep you company."

Devra took a deep breath and crossed her legs tighter. "Does it make me greedy to dream that could even be a remote possibility?"

"Yes. And there's nothing wrong with wanting as much

happiness as you can find for yourself as long as it's not at someone else's expense." Nola grinned. "It's a solid bet Quinn would enjoy an arrangement like that. As for Trevon, well, you know him better than us."

Except she didn't. Not when it came to these things, because they'd never discussed it. Had actively avoided it, actually. "I need to talk to him. It's going to be a difficult conversation, but you're right. We have to address the situation soon."

"Look, our lifestyle isn't meant for everyone. I'm just saying there are more flavors out there to choose from than being single or married to one man. Feel free to tell your husband about what we've shared, too. I'm sure any of our guys would be willing to sit down and answer his questions if he's not comfortable asking Quinn about it. Because I'm going to be honest..." Sally looked around at her friends.

None of them objected.

So she continued, "We're nervous. Quinn is practically our little brother as much as he is Roman's. He has been in a funk lately, and all of a sudden he's chipper and even maybe kind of hyper. Like a guy who's...infatuated. I'm not sure what's going on between you three, and I'm not sure any of you do either. I think you'd be lying to yourselves if you didn't admit it has the potential to be *something*. Something great. But if you're not careful, it could be a disaster, too. We don't want to see Quinn hurt. Or you. Or Trevon. Please, really take some time to reflect on what you want and don't be afraid to ask for what you need. If Trevon truly loves you, he'll listen with an open mind and a gracious heart."

That's exactly what Devra was afraid of. He was so kind and generous. He'd already sacrificed so much for her. Maybe it was time she accepted responsibility for her part in that and told him it was time for him to take instead of always giving.

She could live with that. He deserved it, even if it didn't involve her. But if it could... That might be the best of both worlds, more than she'd ever dreamed possible. "You ladies are four lucky bitches, you know that?"

"So we've been told." Sally grinned.

"No matter what happens, we're here if you need to talk," Kaelyn promised. "Relationships are complicated, and ours more so than most. We're good listeners. You'll have to be too if you want this to turn out okay."

Devra nodded. "I'm going to try my best. Thank you."

She meant it. For opening her eyes and for offering to be there if she crashed and burned while trying to sort things out. She just hoped no one got too badly hurt. Herself included.

12

Devra left the spa a whole new woman. Physically she looked different, spiffed up with a bright red manicure and her hair styled. She'd even been talked into wearing some bolder makeup by the Hot Rods women, who'd sworn she looked amazing. She felt different, too, refreshed and invigorated. Mentally, she was as far away from where she'd been that morning as her hometown was from Middletown. She felt enlightened and ready to conquer the world, starting with her own backyard. Or bedroom.

As if the Hot Rods had done the same for her insides as the masseuse had done for her muscles, Devra's guts had unknotted for the first time in years, since she'd entangled Trevon in this mess. He was too decent for his own good.

It wasn't going to be easy to approach him for a mature, frank, and empathetic discussion about their issues after trying to ignore them for so long. It was the only way out, though. For them both.

She owed him that much at least.

So Devra had asked Sally to drop her off at the end of the long Hot Rides driveway in order to gather her thoughts and prepare for what was to come on the stroll through the quiet, moonlit woods. To make sure she expressed herself in a way that was genuine and respectful, without getting upset or losing control of her emotions no matter what Trevon had to say in response.

A warm glow spilled from the two neighboring tiny homes onto the narrow stretch of grass separating them, illuminating it twice as brightly where the light overlapped. She stood there for a minute or two, staring at that spot. What if the things the Hot Rods women had said could be true for her and Trevon, too? Could they burn twice as bright if they were open to unconventional possibilities?

Devra wondered what Quinn was doing inside and what he might think of the details his friends had disclosed. Still, she didn't allow herself to waver from her original goal: Trevon.

She'd gotten back a lot later than originally anticipated since the ladies had taken her out to eat after they'd finished at the spa. Devra thought they had been not-so-secretly making sure she was okay and had time to process everything they'd told her before they unleashed her on her poor unsuspecting husband. They'd texted Quinn, who'd relayed the message to Trevon. He'd told her to have fun and not to rush.

Apparently the guys had been working late at the shop, fixing up Pop's bike. That should have put Trevon in a good mood, at least.

He'd obviously waited up for her. She took that as a sign.

She climbed the three wooden stairs to the tiny home

and let herself in, being careful not to slam the front door of this place she appreciated so much. With its whitewashed shiplap and cornflower blue accents, it was cozy and adorable. Bonus, it was also quick to clean from top to bottom. It had everything they needed without being too much. The combo kitchen and living space accounted for most of the ground floor, with an efficient bathroom tucked behind it. Although nothing inside was grandiose, it was still extremely comfortable, well-designed, and covered in high-end finishes. Quinn had explained that when you only needed three square feet of tile, you could afford to splurge.

Devra couldn't believe this was really their home now. A place they could call their own. As long as what she was about to do didn't ruin everything.

What if it did? At least she wouldn't be living in constant fear that someday Trevon would wake up and decide he'd had enough of her. Some part of her questioned if he'd made that mistake on her green card application because subconsciously he wasn't ready for them to be that permanently attached.

Okay, so that was probably ridiculous, but she still couldn't help the doubts from creeping in.

It was time to stop this madness. If he really was still awake. He hadn't called out a hello to her, so maybe he had fallen asleep with the light on. Wouldn't be the first time. He worked so hard and wore himself out. Devra put extra effort into approaching quietly in case he'd drifted off while reading or something.

A bookcase doubled as a ladder leading up to the lofted platform above the kitchen and bathroom that cradled a ridiculously comfortable foam bed beneath a vaulted ceiling made up of the exposed rafters, which had been painted white. Quinn had strung some LED fairy lights around the loft that made it seem magical and romantic. Not at all like the bachelor pad she might have expected of the teenager he'd been when he'd built this place with the help of the Powertools crew.

Devra took a deep breath, then boosted herself onto the first shelf-rung. It creaked when Trevon climbed it, but he was easily twice her size. She went up slowly, careful not to misplace a foot and knock anything off. That would probably scare the shit out of Trevon. He'd bolt upright in bed and smack his head on one of those pretty beams. Not the way she wanted to begin their talk.

So when her eyes cleared the platform, she peeked at the bed they shared night after night while keeping as much space down the middle as possible, each of them curled up tight on their respective sides.

Devra hated that gap that she couldn't seem to bridge. But if it hurt her to lie next to him without cuddling, speaking soft words, or making love, well, that was her problem, not his. He'd never promised her more than a safe haven, which he'd delivered.

What she saw wasn't at all what she expected.

Trevon was very definitely awake. In fact, he was woke all over.

Her eyes flew open wide and she nearly lost her grip on the bookcase, which would have resulted in her crashing to the ground below and ruining the very intimate moment for Trevon.

So she clung tight. And couldn't stop staring.

No wonder he hadn't greeted her. He appeared extremely distracted by whatever he was watching on the tablet Quinn had lent them. Was that...pornography?

The soft moans and the sound of skin slapping skin

that began to come from the device seemed to support her theory.

It was then she realized that Trevon was holding the tablet with one hand while the other had slipped beneath the sheet covering him up to his waist. The tent made by his erection was obvious even from her vantage point. She'd never seen a naked man before Trevon, and only a few times when he'd been coming out of the shower or changing clothes, but she wondered if all of them were as big as he was. She guessed not.

What she saw shocked her. Yet it fascinated her, too.

She should go. Or at least back up a few steps and make sure he knew she was there.

Except she couldn't look away. The gentleman who'd sacrificed so much for her was sprawled on the bed, making it seem much smaller than she knew it was.

His hand added to the bulk under the sheet, moving in slow strokes for a bit before he shifted and the sheet fell away from his groin. Devra stared, utterly frozen by curiosity and...desire. She licked her lips as his hand began to move faster, pumping up his shaft, making it harder and darker.

She'd never seen it erect before, never mind *that* hard. Impressive even when he was getting out of the shower or changing clothes, now it was big enough that she gulped.

She should leave.

But she couldn't stop staring at her husband and the things he was doing to himself. It looked like it felt so damn good. Why hadn't he let her do this for him? Was it because she didn't have experience and didn't know how to do it right?

He could have taught her. She would have enjoyed putting that look of pure rapture on his face.

What was he thinking about when he paused, his eyes scrunched closed so tightly as he worked himself like that —rough, fast, and a little desperate now?

Should she climb the rest of the bookcase and offer to take care of him?

He'd done the same for her in so many ways aside from the physical, it seemed like hardly anything to trade. And part of her would love to...if only things were different between them. If only it wouldn't seem like some crazy obligation to both of them.

No, she couldn't. Not until they'd talked. And this didn't seem like the right time anymore.

Devra bit her lip. Hard. Still, she didn't retreat.

When he paused and reached up to brush the pad of his calloused thumb over his nipple, she realized her hand was mimicking his. She pinched the rock-hard tip of her breast, clapping her other hand over her mouth to keep from hissing at the contact. In her country, she could probably be put to death for spying on a man like this. For what she was watching and the things it made her want.

Here, she didn't care. She needed to see what he was doing and how he could make himself feel good so maybe someday she could do it for him. Or for Quinn. Or maybe for both.

Devra's head tipped to the side as the sounds coming from the tablet escalated and she realized that there were two distinct performers. Both moaning and murmuring nasty things to each other. Both male.

Her heart sped up and her hands grew damp. This time not in such a good way. Maybe this was why Trevon hadn't let her touch him. Maybe she wasn't what he wanted.

She'd suspected that could be, especially after how he'd been acting around Quinn, but...

Had she almost made a complete fool of herself?

Devra trembled, her fingers going back to the bookcase to hold herself steady.

Trevon's hand wandered back down his chest and the ripped muscles of his abs. He cupped his balls and rolled them around in his palm, then trailed his fingers over the taut skin there before allowing himself to take hold of his cock again.

He lifted it off his body. It looked heavy and full.

A groan escaped him, rivaling the ones coming from the movie he was watching, as he wrapped his hand around it and began to pump with more purpose this time. His thumb swiped across the tip, spreading fluid that made it glisten in the low light.

What would it taste like? What would he feel like if it were her fingers around him?

Devra doubted she'd be able to clasp him with just one hand. It would take two. She would surround him and stroke him until he shuddered as he was now. Sweat began to form on his brow and his legs grew restless beneath the sheet.

His hand sped up, working himself faster and faster.

It didn't take long before he seemed strung as tight as a bow ready to fire an arrow.

And when one of the men on the video cried out in ecstasy, followed shortly by his partner echoing him, Trevon's entire body froze, clenched, then bucked. His hips thrust upward and his erection jutted out from the end of his fist.

A stream of pearly seed launched from his cock and splattered on his chest. He grunted and flexed in a primal display of passion that Devra thought was beautiful and somewhat frightening all at once.

Forbidden and exquisite. Raw and real.

As the fluid hit and spread over his muscles, he cried out, "Quinn!"

That one word lanced Devra's heart.

It ripped away any shred of confidence she'd had. Thank God she hadn't made a fool of herself after all. She tore her gaze from her gorgeous husband and the pain that she was causing him by keeping him from what he really craved. It was only then she realized how much he'd given up by marrying her. She was ruining his life, and she didn't know what else to do.

Devra scurried down the bookcase ladder, crossed to the front door, opened and shut it with a bang, then dashed into the bathroom. She closed the door on Trevon, the sham they had been living, and the possibility of making their marriage a real one.

She locked herself inside before stripping off her clothes. With a flick of her wrist, she turned on the water to the hottest setting before sinking to the floor beneath the spray and crumpling into a ball. It scorched her back as it also flattened the pretty waves of her silly hairdo. She tipped her face up into the water and let the makeup drip off her cheeks and swirl the drain before disappearing. It didn't make her feel any cleaner. Not even after she'd stayed there long enough to cry her eyes out.

Who had she been kidding? She wasn't a seductress. And even if she had been, it wouldn't have made her desirable to her husband. He needed things she couldn't give him. He craved the touch of a man.

No matter how much she wanted to set him free, she needed him to keep her close to survive.

How was she going to make this right? She was terrified she couldn't. At least not while ensuring her own heart and soul remained intact.

Because it was clear to her now that she was on the verge of losing her husband.

Devra loved Trevon, and she didn't want to give him up even if that's what was best for him. She had to let him go, but she couldn't.

Which made her the most selfish, disgusting woman in the world.

13

Quinn looked up from the engine he was rebuilding and saw Devra approaching, her long black hair shining as the breeze stirred it behind her. She was carrying the cobalt blue tray that was starting to elicit a Pavlovian response from him. He smiled and called to Trevon, "Hey, man. Look sharp. Your wife is incoming. I think she's bringing us some lunch."

There were a lot of things he liked about having Devra and Trevon around Hot Rides, but he had to admit her homemade meals was one of his favorites.

"Do you think she made falafels? I swear I could eat them every day and never get tired of her. Them, I mean." Quinn rushed to correct his slip of tongue. His crass thoughts were getting harder to keep to himself, though. He'd been walking around with a perma-boner for days, making him think ruefully of those ED pill commercials that warned about prolonged erections.

Hopefully he wasn't causing permanent damage downstairs.

"I think she said she was doing shakshouka today, but that was yesterday. Now who knows?" Trevon trailed off.

"Even better." Quinn rose from his crouch and wiped his hands on his jumpsuit. Trevon kept working. So he kicked the bottom of the other guy's boot with just enough force to get his attention. "Dude, let's go."

Trevon didn't look up from what he was doing. He muttered, "Be there in a minute."

That was weird. Usually he was racing Quinn to the break room, especially when Devra made shakshouka. It was his favorite.

"Suit yourself. Don't come crying if I polish it all off before you can get some, though. I don't have much self-control when it comes to your wife. Her cooking." Quinn figured he'd better just go eat before he put his foot in his mouth again. Devra's food tasted a lot better than dirty boots.

He turned and met her on the walkway, scooping the tray from her and carrying it the rest of the way. "Damn, Devra. This smells even better than yesterday's lunch."

"Thanks." She didn't smile when she said it.

"Everything okay?" he asked as he opened the door and held it for her to enter first.

She seemed reluctant to join him, looking into the garage for her husband. "Yes. Where's Trevon?"

"Working." Quinn rolled his eyes. "His boss must be a total asshole."

Devra did look up then, shaking her head. "He's definitely not. It must be important, though, or Trevon would be in here, spending time with you."

"You mean eating this amazing food, right?" Quinn was kidding around. He snagged a plate and some silverware from the cabinet and dug in. "What is this?"

He pointed to a plate stacked with triangles of fried dough.

"Potato and cheese sambusa," she said, her voice devoid of its usual sparkle.

He had to do something drastic to make her laugh, or crack a smile, something. This side of her was one he didn't know and it sort of alarmed him. Quinn plucked one up, popped it in his mouth whole, and groaned in genuine delight as the flavors of onions, cilantro, and a familiar custom spice mix he'd learned she called hawaij, burst over his tongue. "Devra, these are so fucking good I could kiss you."

Her gaze flicked to his barely long enough for him to realize how panicked her eyes were before returning to the ground.

What. The. Fuck.

Had he overstepped? Made her uncomfortable because Trevon wasn't around? Or maybe because she was more conservative and innocent than most people he knew? Before he could figure it out, she bolted.

"I'd better go. I'll come back later for the dishes." She was already several steps away when he had an idea.

"Don't worry about that. I'll wash them and return them to you this evening. It's the least I can do." Quinn had also bought a bunch of groceries he planned to haul across the yard with the dishes. He was eating enough for three people. Didn't seem right for her and Trevon to pay for it all and do the work of preparing and serving it, too.

"Maybe it'd be better if I send Trevon over to get them." She wrung her hands and said, "He likes spending time with you. You two should do guy stuff after work, you know? Without me."

Uhhhh. Quinn wasn't sure what was going on, but he

could tell he was missing something. "Um, okay. But you're welcome to hang out with us, too."

"I think he needs more time alone. Or, away from me, I guess. Maybe I'll go to Hot Rods and see what the ladies are up to while you two work on Pop's bike or do... whatever. I'll make sure I call before I come back."

"Okay, Devra. Whatever you want. I know the Hot Rods would be happy to have you over." Quinn scratched his jaw, puzzled.

"Of course." She didn't say *you're welcome*. "Enjoy."

She turned to go as Trevon was coming through the door. When their chests might have touched in the close quarters, she swerved in a move worthy of a contortionist to avoid coming in contact with her husband.

"You sure you don't want to eat with us?" Trevon asked her, putting out a hand to keep her from crashing into the wall after her drastic maneuver.

"Positive." She dodged that, too, then spun on her heel and marched away, head down.

"What's up with her?" Quinn asked Trevon.

Trevon shrugged. "I'm not sure. She's been acting super weird since she got back from the spa with the Hot Rods ladies last night. What the hell happened there? I assumed they were going to do girly stuff and bitch about their husbands or some shit."

"Oh fuck." Quinn threw down his fork. Delicious food stuck in his throat. Trevon was right. That's probably exactly what they had done. "There are some things you should know..."

He probably should have briefed Trevon about his friends but they'd gotten so busy talking about heavy subjects and after that, they'd chased away the negative energy by working on the Indian. To Quinn, the Hot Rods and their unconventional relationships were normal. He hadn't thought about how uncomfortable it might make someone with Devra's upbringing to be around them.

"They're not like serial killers or something, right?" Trevon rocked back in his chair without putting a morsel on his plate. He locked his fingers over his stomach as if it hurt. "What the hell is going on?"

"They're amazing people." Quinn promised. "You know how Devra says you saved her life, well, they saved mine. It's just that they're...uh..."

"What?" Trevon asked.

"Polyamorous." Quinn still felt defensive and apprehensive telling someone new about their lifestyle. Because what if Trevon judged them? Then he'd be judging Quinn, too, without even knowing it.

"They're married, though, right?" Trevon narrowed his eyes. He did say he'd seen a few episodes of the *Hot Rods* reality show. Of course, the network didn't exactly air orgies, but...

"Yes, they are. They also share an incredible bond as a group. Well, in a lot of different ways. Mustang Sally is married to Alanso, but Eli is their partner as well. They're a triad. And they and the other couples sometimes party together, if you know what I mean." Quinn wanted Trevon to understand it wasn't only about sex. "They had rough lives. And they came to rely on each other. Love each other. The things they enjoy also make them feel..."

"Whole. Part of something. Secure." Trevon nodded. "I could see that. Fuck. That sounds..."

Quinn prayed he didn't say something like *disgusting, fucked up,* or *immoral* next.

"Hot as hell." He swiped his hand over his face as if it really had gotten twenty degrees warmer in there. "Can I ask...Sally, Eli, and Alanso. How does that work? Does she have two men or are they also—"

"Lovers?" Quinn supplied.

Trevon nodded. "Yeah, that."

"Oh, definitely." He figured it was time to come clean. Hell, he knew Trevon had a thing for men. Maybe he wanted the best of both worlds, too. "They love Sally and they get off on driving her wild, but there's also something between them. Something really powerful."

"Why are you saying it like that?" Trevon wondered. "Like it hurts you."

"Because they make me jealous. I love the idea of what they have. I'm bisexual and I enjoy having two partners, a man and a woman. If I could find my own relationship like theirs I'd consider myself the luckiest man alive."

There. He'd admitted it. And he couldn't take it back. Didn't even want to.

Trevon stood up so fast, his chair scraped against the concrete loud enough to make them both jump. "I better go see if Devra's okay."

Quinn wasn't trying to be a perv, but he couldn't help but notice the giant bulge in Trevon's jumpsuit. It was right there, at eye level. He gripped the table as hard as he could to keep from lunging across it and ripping down the zipper to see it and suck it without those layers of bulky canvas and denim in between them.

"Yeah. Yeah, you should." Quinn needed a few minutes to himself, too.

He watched Trevon run down the driveway toward their tiny homes, then went into the garage and flipped the sign from *Open* to *Closed*. He trudged back into the break room and piled his plate high with Devra's exceptional food.

Damn if he would let her efforts go to waste. Besides, in some weird way, consuming the meal she'd cooked made him feel closer to her, warmed from the inside out.

Hopefully she wouldn't be so cold next time they ran into one another.

If she was—or worse, if Trevon took her and left Hot Rides for good—Quinn would be crushed.

14

Trevon crashed through the door, then froze when he saw Devra braced against the kitchen counter on straight-locked arms. Her head was bowed, her hair curtaining her face. But her sobs were plain despite the fact that he couldn't see the tears falling from her beautiful eyes.

Even when they'd gotten the news of her father's demise, he hadn't seen her break down like this. She'd wept, of course, but had been more stoic and almost resigned. This was...pure panic and heartbreak. What had hurt her and how could he make it better?

"Devra," he groaned, crossing to her then stopping a few feet short before he could gather her in his arms and tuck her against his chest. He wanted nothing more than to hold her and rock her until they both calmed down and could hash things out.

Would she welcome his touch in such a vulnerable moment?

Probably not.

Maybe, if they could get beyond the barriers they'd

learned to construct around these deep wounds they held inside, they could start to make some progress in their relationship. Trevon crooned, "Devra, honey. Don't cry. Everything's going to be okay."

"It's not!" She flung her head back, her hair whipping around, so she could glare at him defiantly. Her eyes burned like molten gold. It was the first time she'd ever shown him this side of her, a fiery side. It did nothing to help his hard-on settle down.

"Okay." He raised his hands, palms out, and held them there. "Tell me what's wrong then. Please? We'll figure out how to get through it together."

"Are you sure that's what you want?" Her beautiful features were twisted in pain that hurt him to see.

"Of course." How could she doubt that after everything they'd endured by each other's sides? He took a step toward her, except she retreated one, her ass bumping into the cabinet in the corner of the tiny-home kitchen.

She had nowhere left to run.

Trevon was at a loss. He wasn't trying to trap her, he just needed to understand what was happening. Maybe Quinn was right. Maybe the Hot Rods had exposed her to things that had shocked her. "What the hell is going on here, Devra? Did you hear or see something last night that upset you?"

"Like you masturbating to fantasies of Quinn?" she asked, deflating before his eyes, clinging to the countertop behind her for support as her knees threatened to buckle. "Yes."

Trevon coughed. Air rushed out of his lungs like it would from a blown tire. He clutched his chest as he bent at the waist, doubled over with the impact of her accusation and the ramifications it would have on their life. He'd tried so hard to suppress those parts of himself so that he could make her happy.

Clearly, he'd failed.

They were both miserable.

"I shouldn't have snooped, I'm sorry, but I checked your browser history, too. You really like to watch gay porn."

She'd done *what*?

"You've been spying on me?" Trevon snarled, feeling like an injured animal, surrounded by hunters.

"It's okay." Devra held her hands up. Tears spilled down her cheeks, calling her a liar. "I'm not judging you. And I'm not mad. I'm more...distressed. Ashamed that I've been holding you back from what you really need. We both know you're only with me out of obligation."

"That's bullshit!" Trevon never got angry. Except for right then. The skin of his face felt like it had touched the exhaust pipe of his bike. Warmth spread down his neck and across his chest.

He wouldn't have been surprised if he began to overheat and steam started pouring out of his ears. It only got worse when she kept spouting such garbage.

"I've been enough of a burden on you already." Devra stood taller then, even if her legs wobbled some as she did. "I'm thinking maybe it's best if I leave so you can be who you were really meant to be. So you can be happy...without me."

"Stop...talking...like that." Trevon hissed between clenched teeth. It was killing him that she thought these things. Where had he fucked up so badly that she didn't realize how much he loved her? "You know I care for you.

You're my best friend and I wouldn't change anything between us."

Devra winced at that. "Really? Because I would."

It caught him off-guard, exactly how much it hurt to hear her say that. "I know things haven't been perfect. I'm doing my best for us, though. With this job and this house—"

Devra silenced him. "That's not what I'm talking about. I mean that I want more, for us both, than a platonic partnership that allows us to get by comfortably. You're obviously craving the same thing—*passion*. And if I'm not the one who can give it to you..."

"How am I supposed to take from you, Devra?" Trevon didn't see how it was possible that he could without feeling like he was abusing their situation. He was her only choice. That wasn't right.

"I know. I get it. I'm not right for you. Quinn seems like he is." She dashed tears from her face with the back of her hands then stared him straight in the eye when she said, "You should go for it. Make a move and see if he's interested. You're an amazing man. You deserve to be happy."

"No." Trevon shook his head and waved his hands in front of his chest. "No way."

"Why wouldn't you want to experience your fantasies if you have the chance?" Devra asked, rocking Trevon's world. "I completely understand, you know. He's sexy. He's responsible. He's empathetic. He's rugged and he's a little bit broken, isn't he? Honestly, I think maybe he needs you as much as I do. Did. I mean *did*."

Trevon couldn't react for a moment, torn in two directions. One path was hopeful and exciting so he went that way first. "You're attracted to Quinn, too?"

When she refused to answer, crossing her arms, he voiced his other thought. "You really don't need me anymore?"

Why did that thought bruise his heart? He liked protecting her. The ragtag team they'd become over the past two years—when it was them against the world—was something he prized. Didn't she?

Devra gave him purpose and made him feel like he was doing something right no matter how terrible the rest of their lives had gotten. Unfortunately, she dodged that question, too.

Instead, she said, "Maybe you need to do some things for yourself more than others right now. And if that's too much for you to handle, then at least do something for Quinn. He needs someone, too."

Trevon didn't like that as she cooled down, her calm rationality was starting to make some sort of sense to him. He didn't want her to be right about this. It confused him that she could be so practical and so willing to let go of what they'd been building between them.

Devra didn't resolve any of the doubts or insecurities she'd raised within him. She sounded tired, utterly wiped out, when she said, "I'm going to Hot Rods for a while. Okay?"

He sure as shit wasn't going to stop her. He wasn't her parent; he was her husband. Her partner, or at least he had thought he was. "Of course. Just...have someone call Quinn when you get there so I know you're safe, please?"

"I'm glad you still care." She brushed fresh moisture from her eyes, then raced over and hugged him. Before he could do the same, she dashed to the door, pausing only to say over her shoulder, "I'm sorry, Trevon. I'm so sorry I did this to you."

Devra took off then, jogging out of sight before he could even figure out what to do. He wandered out onto the porch to keep her in sight a few moments more, cursed, then kicked the post next to the stairs. Even with his boots on, the impact radiated up his leg.

"Careful, neighbor," came a soft warning from next door. *Quinn. Fuck.*

Trevon didn't think he was ready to face the man and come clean about the big blowup he'd just had with his wife. Not caused by something Quinn's friends had done after all, but because of his own dumbass judgment and the outlet he'd chosen for his pent-up desires.

"I didn't mean to eavesdrop, but I couldn't sit up in the garage knowing you two were fighting and, well..." Quinn gestured to the tiny strip of grass between the cottages.

Oh fuck. How much had he heard? Trevon tried to replay their argument in his mind.

It was pretty damning.

"Is it true?" Quinn asked. "What she said? About last night?"

Of course it was, but was Trevon ready to admit it?

All this subterfuge and burying of issues was what was causing their problems. If he wanted any hope of digging out of the mess he'd made, he'd have to come clean. To Quinn. And to his wife.

"Yeah." He scrubbed his hand over his face.

Quinn tracked the movement as if he was studying Trevon's fingers and picturing what they would look like wrapped around the erection still making an obvious bulge in his pants at that moment despite—or maybe enhanced by—the endorphins, adrenaline, and salacious thoughts his shouting match with Devra had stirred up.

"Do you plan to follow through on what she

suggested?" Quinn wondered, idly leaning one shoulder against his own porch support, his hands jammed in his pockets as if Trevon's response didn't matter. But Devra had been right about that at least.

Quinn wasn't whole either. Trevon could tell because he recognized fractured parts of himself in the other guy. Devra obviously was cracked, too. They were a matched set, the three of them.

So he chose his words carefully. "I would like to, if there weren't consequences."

"I wouldn't pick me over her either." Quinn barked out a laugh. It rang false. Hollow. Not at all like the genuine amusement they'd shared during long days at Hot Rides.

"It's not like that," Trevon promised. "I'm married. Whether or not Devra believes it, I meant every word of the vows I took with her. I love her. I just..."

"You're stuck." Quinn nodded. "I know. You told me. I have to be honest, Trevon. If Devra hadn't just gone apeshit on you, I would."

"What?" Trevon hadn't expected that. Some friend Quinn was. He threw his hands up. "Why?"

"Were you listening to what she said?" Quinn crossed the lawn to stand next to Trevon. "I heard her shout that she wanted things to be different. She's tired of only being your *best friend*. She's afraid you don't want her because you're gay and that she's stifling you by being married to her."

"Oh." Trevon plopped onto the top stair. He thought about it carefully from Quinn's perspective, taking a minute or more to rehash their argument. "She sort of did imply that, didn't she?"

His head spun.

"If you don't fuck your wife soon, you are going to end

up losing her." Quinn put his hand on Trevon's shoulder.

He scrunched his eyes closed. "I'm not good at this. You've known her for a week and you can read her better than me. I'm afraid that if we cross that line, I'll be taking advantage. What if she changes her mind but I'm so lost in the moment, in finally having her, that I don't see it? I would never forgive myself."

"That's not going to happen. But..." Quinn hesitated. He swallowed hard, then shook his head as if he wasn't going to finish his thought.

"What?" Trevon turned toward Quinn and put his hand on the other guy's knee. He squeezed, surprised when Quinn's calf clenched tight at the contact. "Please. What? I need help."

"If you're seriously so worried that it will prevent you from ever taking that next step with her, and if you also think it might calm her nerves about you being bisexual and what that means for your marriage, I'd be willing to—"

Trevon's mind was instantly flooded with new, much wilder fantasies than what he'd been thinking of the night before. He reflected on what Quinn had told him about the Hot Rods and how they rolled. Yes. Yes, it could work. "If she was up for it, you'd make love to Devra with me? At least for the first time? Her first time. *Our* first time."

It was an outlandish idea, but it might be exactly what they needed.

"Think of me as more of a sexy chaperone." Quinn shrugged as if it didn't matter, though Trevon knew the stakes were high for all three of them. What Quinn was volunteering to do was dangerous for him, too. He would be an outsider and there wasn't much upside other than fleeting pleasure for him.

"*If* we do this..." Trevon looked up at Quinn. "You need to swear that you're not going to blame yourself if shit doesn't work out. You're right. It's kind of a last-ditch effort at this point. But if we don't do something drastic, we're not going to make it. So if we try, and it still doesn't work out, that's not on you. Got it?"

"Yeah." Quinn nodded, but his mouth was set in a tight slash that made Trevon wonder if he really meant it.

This was either the best or worst idea he'd ever had, and he wouldn't know which until it was too late to change his mind. "Okay then. How are we going to do this?"

"Simple. We're going to seduce your wife. First, you've got to talk to her and make sure we're not ambushing her. She has to agree up front, without us pressuring her into it once she's turned on." Quinn was serious about that and Trevon agreed. They wouldn't do anything unless that's what Devra wanted, too.

"I hope you're right about this." Trevon kept replaying the moment Devra said she would change things between them if it was up to her. Maybe this was exactly what she'd needed from him and hadn't been getting. He also couldn't stop thinking about how adamant she'd been that he experiment with Quinn.

Maybe they both would get what they needed. Maybe this could save them.

"I am." Quinn's smile brightened up the shadows that had been lurking inside Trevon for a while now as he gripped Trevon's shoulder tighter and shook him a bit. "Thank you for trusting me. This is going to be amazing."

"Somehow, I believe you." Trevon couldn't decide if he was a fool or a genius.

But he was going to find out soon enough.

15

Quinn hung out with Trevon for a few hours, doing some more work on the Indian to take their minds off the shit about to go down. Eventually, they gave up. It was impossible not to think about what might lie ahead.

"I'm going to go see my brother and Tom. I'll bring Devra home whenever she's ready, okay?" Quinn asked.

Trevon nodded and turned toward the cottage. "Thanks."

"No problem." Quinn couldn't help but tease him a little. "If you want to jerk off over my hotness, try to do it quick so she doesn't bust you this time, cool?"

Trevon shot him the finger, but his laughter was clear through the steamy, late afternoon air.

Quinn grinned as he got on his motorcycle and breathed easier himself. He took the long way to Hot Rods and had mostly settled down, his mind clearer, when he rolled up behind the shop. He looked up above the garage and saw lights on but decided he needed to get Tom's opinion first.

Tom was his surrogate father and not part of the complex poly relationship the rest of their family-by-choice had going on. If he thought Quinn was doing the right thing, then that was the gold standard test.

Quinn clomped up the stairs to the door and rapped once, hard, since he'd walked in on Tom and his bride more than once and never wanted to do it again.

He'd gotten trained to knock early on in his stay at Hot Rods both at the main house and definitely at his brother's place above the garage.

"Get in here, Quinn," Tom shouted. "We've got some shit to talk about."

Figured. Word traveled fast in Middletown, and lightning fast among his circle of friends.

He was shaking his head as he made his way into the kitchen, not too surprised to see his brother Roman already there. In front of Tom and Roman on the table was a laptop. That could only mean one thing. They were talking about him with some of their other friends who lived out of state.

The Powertools crew.

Well, shit. There was no escaping now. At least Quinn would have plenty of feedback, from people he trusted, about what he was about to do. They would have no problem telling him straight up if he was letting his dick do the thinking in this situation.

At least that gave him some peace of mind. If nothing else, he wanted to be sure that Devra and Trevon didn't get hurt anymore by what he'd proposed. He cared about them and wanted them to make it out of this happy and whole. If he couldn't have a perfect relationship for himself, he at least wanted to see those around him make it work so that he knew it was possible

—someday—for him to find the right people to love him.

Maybe. There was a dark sliver that thought he might just be unlovable. Even his own mother hadn't been able to care for him like she should have.

Quinn shook that thought off as he sat beside Roman. Sure enough, a random collection of the Powertools crew were on screen, lounging on the massive sectional in Kayla and Dave's cabin at their mountain resort.

"Hey." He waved to Dave, Kayla, Mike, Joe, and Devon. The rest of the crew might be within earshot, though he couldn't see them onscreen at the moment. "Any little ears around I need to worry about?"

"Nah. Abby, Nathan, Klea, and Landry are outside with Morgan, Kate, and my guys," Devon told him. The four crew kids were getting bigger every time he saw them. Hell, Abby was going to turn ten soon. He couldn't believe time was going by so quickly. It made him realize he was letting too many chances go to find his own forever person, or people.

"So cut the crap and get right to the good stuff." Mike, the foreman of the Powertools construction crew leaned forward. "What's going on with those two at your shop? We met Devra earlier when she was hanging out with the Hot Rods ladies. She seems pretty fucking great. And cute, too. So why did it look like she'd been crying her damn eyes out?"

"They're married. And they're having issues." Quinn shrugged one shoulder. That's the simplest way he could summarize it.

"What kind of issues?" Kayla asked.

Tom and Roman were staring at Quinn along with their friends on the other side of the internet connection.

He cleared his throat, then explained, "Trevon is bisexual. He has a crush on me..."

"Which is mutual, I presume," Dave said.

Quinn nodded. "Fuck yes. If you think Devra is cute— which is bullshit because she's gorgeous—you should see him. He's...anyway..."

If he didn't quit thinking about that, he'd end up a lot more uncomfortable than he already was. Roman was grinning at him and Tom was masking a smile with his palm.

"Even though they're married and they're hot as hell, both of them, they've never had sex together. Devra, likely never at all for that matter." Quinn dropped the bomb and braced himself for the million questions that would follow.

"What?" Devon's eyes grew wide.

"Why not?" Mike wondered.

Dave stood up, lurching a little on his bad leg, which stiffened when he sat too long. "Quinn, are you getting yourself entangled in too much drama here? You don't need that in your life."

"I feel like...I can help them. That's not stupid, is it?" Quinn honestly needed to know.

"Yes. It probably is." Roman knocked his knee lightly into Quinn's. "But why do you think that?"

"Devra thinks she's an obligation to Trevon. He married her in part so she could stay here instead of having to move back to Yemen after her father was killed. It's not safe for her there. And of course Trevon did protect her, but he also loves her. I can see it every time he looks at her. They're best friends and could be so much more. Trevon is afraid to show her that because he feels like she's stuck with him and didn't have a choice. It's all so fucked up. And then, yesterday, Devra walked in on Trevon having a private moment with himself…"

"Jerking off?" Joe asked. "So what?"

Tom was muttering about kids today and over-sharing, but he didn't stop Quinn from finishing the story. "He sort of, uh, called my name when… you know."

Everyone groaned in unison.

"Yeah. Exactly." Quinn planted his elbows on the table and buried his face in his hands.

"So that poor girl thinks her husband is only married to her because it was the right thing to do, but that he's really into guys and not her, otherwise he surely would have fucked her senseless by now. Right?" Kayla put her hand over her mouth. "I'd cry, too. She obviously really loves him or she wouldn't care that she's hurting him by staying married when she has no other choice. This really is messed up."

Tom leaned forward so he could meet Quinn's gaze. "How exactly are you going to help them?"

"By having sex with them." Okay, it didn't sound like such an awesome plan in this context, but it had made sense to him earlier.

Tom simply kept staring. "I don't get it. Are you sure you've thought this through, or is this some excuse to get what you want that you're going to regret later?"

He didn't say it, but Quinn heard the *like that time you slept with your girlfriend's brother* that remained unspoken.

"Hang on, Tom." Roman came to Quinn's rescue as always. "I sort of think it makes sense. You're trying to get them past this mental roadblock they have so they can see they're compatible and meant to be much more than friends. Plus, you're going to enjoy the hell out of it for the moment."

"But long-term..." Tom was still confused.

"There is no long-term plan." Quinn shrugged. "I just want to help. To make things right and maybe, yes, to atone for that time I pushed people apart instead of bringing them together."

"You're going to sacrifice your own happiness?" Joe frowned. "I'm not sure this is a good idea, Quinn. Yes, you can help them. But you need to think about what's best for yourself, too. If you care about them, and I think you do, in addition to being attracted to them..."

"This is going to end up biting you in the ass." Mike might as well have hit him over the head with a two-by-four. "You're going to get hurt."

Probably true.

That wasn't going to stop him from doing it anyway. "At least it'll feel good for tonight. Or...whenever they take me up on it. If they do."

Tom scowled. "I don't like this."

Roman looked between Tom, the Powertools crew, and then Quinn. "Sometimes you have to take a risk. Yes, you might get burned. But...there's something here. I haven't seen you like this, well, ever. They're calling to you and you've been trying so hard to keep yourself away from that kind of real feeling for years now. I think it'll be good for you. Even if it hurts."

"Spoken like a true Dom, huh?" Devon teased Roman. "Is that what you tell Carver when you're about to beat his ass?"

Tom put his hands over his ears. "Okay, over the line! Don't talk about my kids like that!"

Of course, that had everyone rolling with laughter. Quinn included.

When the ruckus had died down and they'd said their

goodbyes to the Powertools, Roman closed the laptop and turned toward Quinn. "You know I'm here if you need me. I don't like the idea of my little brother getting his heart broken, but if it happens...I'm here."

If he answered seriously, Quinn might have choked up. So he said, "I'm not exactly your little brother anymore."

"When I'm eighty fucking years old, you'll still be my little brother. Get used to it." Roman smirked.

Tom snorted. "Yeah, and I'll still be your dad. Both of you. So here's what I want you to know. You've screwed around plenty, but you've never taken a relationship seriously. That needs to change right now if you're really going to do this. You need to be in it all the way. Half-assed isn't going to do the three of you any good."

Quinn nodded, and realized that's what had him so twisted up inside. There were consequences to these decisions and actions. It wasn't something he could do and forget.

Even if Trevon and Devra never knew it, this wasn't going to be a fling for him.

It meant more.

He prayed he could help them as much as they might be able to help him.

"Well then, what are you waiting for?" Tom pointed to the Hot Rods garage. "That girl needs a ride home so she can sort things out with her husband. Take her to him. And good luck."

Roman hugged Quinn then shoved him toward the door. "Go."

So he did. Quinn jogged across the lawn and up the metal, open-backed stairs to the Hot Rods' apartment. When he opened the door, he was greeted by Buster

McHightops. Behind him was Devra, leaning against the kitchen island.

"Hey," he said. He didn't bother asking if she was okay, because it was clear that she wasn't. "Ready to go home?"

She shrugged. "I don't know."

He had the urge to hug her. To promise it was going to work out. But that wasn't his place.

At best, he was some sort of sexy mediator. He had to remember that he didn't get to claim either of his two new friends as his own. They belonged to each other. He was only there to help them work out their problems.

He swallowed his disappointment and held his hand out to Devra. "Come on. It's not going to get any better until you talk to Trevon."

She paused, then nodded, putting her fingers in his. He couldn't help but brush his thumb over her soft skin. He wasn't a fucking saint, okay?

"Is he mad?" Devra asked.

"No. Just worried about you and what's going to happen." Quinn could squelch her worries about that anyway.

"Did...um...anything happen after I left?" Her question came out like a croak.

While it might be fun to tease her under normal circumstances, there was too much wrapped up in this situation for jokes. "We worked on the bike. Kept our hands to ourselves and talked about you the whole time."

"Oh." Devra heaved a huge sigh as he drew her to the door and then downstairs. He escorted her toward his motorcycle. "I'm not sure if I should be relieved or upset that we're still...frozen in place."

Quinn turned toward her and helped her onto his motorcycle. Damn, she looked fine on it. He might have a new fantasy or twenty of his own after this. It was going to be the best sort of torture to drive her home. To Trevon.

"About that...I think Trevon has some things he'd like to discuss with you. A plan, maybe." Quinn didn't feel comfortable saying more than that.

"That the two of you cooked up while I was gone?" Devra raised a brow at him, making him grin despite the circumstances. She was like an angry pixie. "Oh boy."

"Exactly." Quinn straddled his motorcycle then started it. He reached behind him to grasp her hands and then flattened them on his abs. She was used to riding with Trevon, so she scooched up closer and plastered herself against him. Her breasts were soft and arms were tight, hugging her to his back.

Yup, pure torture. Because now it was all too easy to imagine what it might feel like if Trevon and Devra agreed to go forward with their scheme.

Quinn drove a little faster than he should have on the way home. Because the sooner they got there, the sooner he'd find out if he would be sleeping alone...again...or if he was about to have the best night of his life.

16

Devra wished Quinn didn't feel so damn good under her fingers. His body flexed and tightened as they sped along the curves of the road he knew so well. The one that linked where he was from to the future he was building. He smelled amazing, too, like leather and gasoline. Combined with the fresh air whipping through her hair, it was intoxicating.

Her husband had good taste in men at least.

She closed her eyes, wondering what it would be like if she was clinging to a man like this in bed. She wanted to ride, with her husband or someone else. She'd waited long enough to feel complete, in touch with all of herself.

Tonight was going to change everything for them. Even if it meant she had to leave the comfort and safety of Trevon's partnership behind. Now that they were out of survival mode, she realized they had a lot of other needs they hadn't considered before.

Quinn roared up the driveway, past Gavyn and Amber's house, then Hot Rides, and finally to their cottages, which sat side by side. As they neared, Trevon must have heard them approaching because he stepped out onto the porch. He didn't have a shirt on.

His bare chest nearly distracted her from the dread about the difficult discussion they were going to have to have. Almost, but not quite.

When she got off the bike and handed Quinn her helmet, he clung to her hand for a few seconds too long. "Hey, just remember, it's going to be okay. You two care for each other and you're trying to do what's best for you both. As long as you're working toward the same goal, you'll figure it out. Okay?"

Devra bit her lip then nodded. "Thanks. For the ride and...everything."

"You're welcome." His bright blue eyes seemed to glow in the twilight. Did she read heat in them or was it her imagination?

Either way, she had to go before she did something completely inappropriate while her husband watched. Her body buzzed with the effects of their close contact on the way here. And probably because she knew what she was about to say to Trevon.

If she could keep her nerve that long.

Devra turned, concentrating on keeping her shoulders back and standing tall as she marched toward her husband. Not prepared for war so much as brutal honesty.

Trevon stuffed his hands in the pockets of his low-riding jeans. "Hey."

"Hey," she parroted. "Can we talk?"

"Of course." He sank onto the slightly uneven boards so that his ass was at the top of the porch and his boots rested a few steps down. Devra sighed and did the same. Except she leaned into his side and laid the edge of her face against his shoulder. He'd been a rock for her during the most turbulent times of her life, and she hadn't given him enough credit for it or realized that maybe he needed her just as much.

Before he could say anything, she whispered, "I'm sorry, Trevon."

"There's nothing for you to apologize for." He put an arm around her, rubbing the bare skin below her sleeve. It was only by the contrast to his warmth that she realized how chilly she'd gotten in the cool evening air. With his free hand, he took her fingers in his and squeezed. "I think you were brave to express how you felt earlier. I regret it came to that and that we didn't talk about it before it became a giant problem for us both."

"I agree, we should try to do better in the future." She hoped there was still a future for them, no matter what it might look like. "Starting now."

"Okay, then there are some things I would like to tell you." Trevon angled his body toward hers so they could look each other in the eye as they shared their deepest secrets and desires. "I'm attracted to both men and women. I don't have a ton of experience, though. I slept with a few women and hooked up with one guy when I was a teenager. It never went further than making out and oral once. So when it comes to that, I'm a virgin, too. I need you to know I've been faithful to you. Since I met you, there hasn't been anyone else I've been interested in until..."

"Quinn." Devra nodded. "Trevon, will it make you feel better or worse if I admit that I'm attracted to him, too?"

His eyes widened as they scanned her questioning gaze. "You are?"

She bit her lip and nodded. "Yeah. He's sexy. Nearly as sexy as you."

"Me?" Trevon's eyebrows were in danger of flipping over the back of his skull.

"I should have told you before now, but yeah, I have pretty big crush on my husband." Devra tried to smile as she said it, but her spine stiffened in case he flung her away from him. "In fact, I love you, Trevon."

"I love you, too, Devra. Please never doubt that. But love and sexual attraction don't have to be connected. Are you sure that you feel both for me?" He winced. "Maybe what you really feel are natural sexual urges and I'm just the guy who happens to be around, married to you, and that's what you believe you're supposed to feel for me."

If he hadn't looked so serious and so exposed in that moment she might have made some wisecrack. Instead, she put her free hand on his knee and began to stroke him to hopefully start soothing some of the hurt she'd unintentionally inflicted on him.

"It's true that I've never felt like this before. I've never been with a man and don't have anything to compare this to, but I want to feel *something*. And want to feel it with you. I trust you. I care for you."

"Those are all awesome things. Seriously. It makes me proud that someone I respect as much as you believes so much in me." Trevon cleared his throat.

"What?" she prodded him. "Be honest, remember? I can handle it. Say what you're thinking."

"I want to make love to you. I want to show you what it's like to experience physical pleasure. You have no idea how much I would enjoy teaching you about your body and the rapture it can bring you." Trevon practically melted her panties off. She'd never seen this side of him before. Romantic, funny, sweet, hardworking, loyal—yes, he was all those things. But seductive?

Never, before now.

"Sounds good to me." Her voice cracked and she didn't even care that he could tell how much his words were impacting her. "But how will that give you what you need too?"

"Because I want to invite Quinn to watch me do it," he said it plainly, as if it wasn't the most outrageous thing he'd ever said to her.

Shivers ran the entire length of Devra's body as she instantly pictured what that might be like. Two gorgeous men worshipping her instead of one. As lucky as Mustang Sally or their friend, Devon. It made her feel powerful in a way she hadn't since she'd been forced to flee and lost everything she'd ever known, including her family and her faith in humanity.

"Would you get off on that, too?" She refused to be selfish about this. He had to enjoy it or she wasn't going to even consider it.

He swallowed hard.

"Be honest. Please. Either way, tell me so we can figure this out," Devra begged. If there was an avenue to save their relationship and still be happy, she wanted to take it. For them both.

"Yes. Son of a bitch, I'm so hard thinking about it." He shifted where he sat, a slight wince cutting across his face.

Devra couldn't say what came over her. She didn't tell herself she shouldn't have the urges she did or refuse to allow herself to give in to them. Instead, she shook her hand free of Trevon's and slowly glided it up his thigh. He didn't stop her. So she cupped the thick length of him, weighing and measuring it for herself.

His cock was even bigger than she'd imagined. Heavier, too.

He groaned when she involuntarily squeezed his shaft. So she pulled away, leaving him breathing hard.

"No. It's okay." He leaned his forehead on hers as if it was too hard to hold his head up. "It just felt...so good."

"Then why haven't we done this before?" She couldn't erase the past two years where he'd kept her at a civil distance from her memory. "You know, the Hot Rods and Powertools ladies told me something wild. Except, the more I think about it, the more I think they might be right."

"Wilder than how they're into threesomes and orgies?" Trevon's eyes nearly popped out of his head.

Devra laughed, then nodded slightly. It was the first hint she had of the man who'd become her best friend and how their lives might transform if they took this next step together. "Yeah. They said that you might feel like *you're* taking advantage of *me*. Because of how we met."

"That's not ridiculous at all. It's fucking true." He put his hands on either side of her face and held it so that she had to look deep into his eyes. She could see the agony there and the indecision. He was as torn about this as she was. But he shouldn't be. She wanted it. Desperately.

"But I want you, Trevon. I always have." She closed her eyes and hoped he knew it was true.

"You didn't have a choice. You didn't pick me." The last words were a mere whisper. One she felt more than heard. And when her eyes fluttered open, she realized he was there. Right there. His lips a hairbreadth from hers.

"I like to consider it destiny." Devra had always assumed divine intervention put them together at precisely the right moments in their lives. But he didn't share her beliefs. Not all of them. And she shouldn't have assumed he would think the same. "Is that why you want

Quinn there? To make sure you're not taking advantage of me?"

"He'll have a clearer mind. He'll stop me if you're not into it. He'll be able to think rationally, which I can't do when I'm around you. And certainly won't be able to do if I'm inside you." He trembled at the thought alone, inspiring her to put her arms around him and hold him close.

She didn't need Quinn to be their safety net—she already knew she was falling for her husband and that he would catch her when she did. But if it made Trevon feel better, and maybe would get him something he needed that she couldn't provide... Devra was in. All in.

"Let's do it. That's what I want. To experience this with you in whatever way it takes to make you comfortable and enjoy it as much as I already know I will. I love you, Trevon. Please, make love to me."

"I'd be honored to, Devra. I love you, too. All I ever want is to make you happy and bring you pleasure. It broke my heart to see you cry today," Trevon whispered. "Let me make it up to you."

And he did.

By sealing their mouths together in the first passionate kiss they'd ever shared.

From the first moment their lips touched, Devra saw stars. She would have sworn there was a meteor shower overhead considering the number of sparks flying through her system.

It was sweet. Achingly gentle. And so damn delicious she knew she'd never get enough of it.

The brush of their tongues against each other in the slightest of contacts made her lean closer into his hold. They sat there, kissing, for long enough that she couldn't catch her breath. If she passed out, so be it—she didn't want to let him go and probably wouldn't have if a blinding spotlight from a wandering flashlight beam hadn't startled them both.

"Oh. Shit. Sorry." Quinn practically stumbled over them where they were making out in the dark. "I didn't see you. Just wanted to make sure everything was okay, but...damn...it looks like it is. So I guess I'll leave you to it. Okay, bye. Have fun."

Devra separated herself from Trevon reluctantly. A riot of laughter belied her euphoric state. How had things gone from utter shit to a fireworks display in a matter of hours?

She didn't know, but she was sure it was going to get even better before the night was done.

With one final look at Trevon, who nodded enthusiastically at her, Devra set their plan in motion. "Quinn, don't go."

He froze, then turned around very slowly. "Why not?"

"Because I'm going to need you to do us a favor tonight." She drew a deep breath. "I'm officially giving that plan you mentioned the green light."

"You are? Both of you?" He looked at her and then Trevon.

They didn't respond verbally. They stood, their hands clasped. Then Devra reached out to him with her free hand and Trevon did the same.

It felt...right. Like fate had steered them here at this very moment.

"Wait, you want to do this tonight? Like...right *now*?" Quinn asked, licking his lips.

"We've waited long enough, don't you think?" Trevon asked.

Devra couldn't agree more, especially after Trevon's kiss had started her engine purring. So she issued the invitation to Quinn. "Will you come in?"

"Hell no." He shook his head, making Trevon hiss and Devra nearly collapse.

Had he changed his mind?

"Why not?" Trevon straightened, like he might rip into Quinn if he'd led them on only to let Devra down. That wasn't how this worked, though. Anyone could say no at any time for any reason. While she appreciated his protectiveness, she wasn't about to let him do something he'd regret later. Devra tugged on his hand to keep him in check.

"If we try to get it on in that loft, someone's going to end up with a broken neck and I'm not going to be responsible for one of those freaky trips to the ER for a sex accident. No way." Quinn tucked the flashlight in his the waistband of his pants, grabbed one of their hands in each of his, and dragged them down the stairs. He walked backward across the lawn separating the cottages as he towed them very willingly along. "We're going to do this right. In my house, and my big, soft bed that's on the main floor of the cottage."

Devra couldn't help but tease her husband. "You're right, Trevon. He's going to make sure no one gets hurt."

Quinn winced at that, and Devra hoped that he was as capable of guarding himself as he was of looking after them. Either way, they weren't stopping now. She was finally going to make love to the man she was married to and give him what they both needed. Hopefully that would make her feel like less of a fraud when she called Trevon her husband.

17

Q uinn should say no. He should turn around and leave this beautiful, fragile couple to resolve their issues on their own instead of allowing them to use him like some sort of sexual crutch. He knew this wasn't the right answer. Or maybe only a temporary solution to their problems.

But he couldn't do it.

He was too fucking self-centered to turn them both down. Still, he felt the need to make sure, with them both there, that everyone was on the same page before he did something he couldn't take back or change. Something that would alter their entire relationship permanently.

Quinn led them into his house, which was about twice the size of the other cottage, though still not grandiose by any standards. When he had them in the living room and Trevon shut the door behind him with a solid click, Quinn tapped in a command on the house's automation system that partially illuminated several strips of LED lights built into the furniture and soffits, lending the whole place a soft glow. It was flattering and allowed them to see each other without the intensity of bright, direct lights. He would have also had the system light the gas fireplace, but it was too damn hot for that already and it would only get steamier as they went.

Trevon looked at him and tipped his head sideways, as if asking how they should proceed.

If Quinn had been intent on having them at any cost, he would have rushed them into the bedroom. But this was different. He cared about how they would feel in the morning, both about themselves and about him. So he spoke clearly and loud enough there could be no misunderstandings. "Tell me again. If you love her and you love him, which that sexy-as-fuck kiss over there made me sure you do... Why the fuck don't you sleep together?"

"We do sleep together. There's only one bed in your other house." Devra swallowed hard. "We just don't have sex in it. Or anywhere. Ever."

Not that Quinn had doubted Trevon, but at least their stories matched and they seemed to be on the same page about where to go from here.

"Tell me why. Each of you. Why haven't you done this before?" Quinn pointed his finger between them. "You know, with each other, not with...a third."

They looked at each other, completely mired in old habits and snarled feelings. Then they spoke simultaneously.

Trevon said, "Because I never want her to feel like she has to have sex with me just because we're married. She doesn't have to pay for her safety with her body."

While Devra said, "Because I never want him to feel like fucking me is his duty. He already went out of his way to keep me here. To keep me safe. I won't force him to give me more of himself than he wants to share."

The couple stared at each other in shock.

Fools. Quinn interrupted their staring match. "You two are too considerate for your own good. You need someone selfish. Someone horny. Someone like me."

Quinn wrestled with his conscience for a few moments longer. Then he thought about what his brother had said. What *all* their friends had said. This was his chance to make a positive change, to bring these two people closer and redress his past transgressions. Instead of ruining their relationship, maybe he could be a bridge. He'd help them close whatever gap there clearly was between them.

Devra looked sidelong at Trevon. He smiled at her and squeezed her hand. They needed this as much as Quinn did.

No—more.

"In that case, I'm glad I bought such a big bed for this place." Quinn smiled, hoping it didn't seem too wolfish. He strode toward the couple until he stood in front of them—not between them—as a third point in some imaginary triangle. He put one hand on the back of each of their necks, using his thumb to rub an arc beneath each of their jaws.

They were unalike and equally alluring.

Devra's skin was soft and silky. It made him want to burrow his face against it and breath deep of the scent—a mix of the delicious spices she cooked with, like cumin and cloves—that always lingered when she'd left the shop.

On the other hand, Trevon's rasped across the pad of his thumb, his stubble giving Quinn extra stimulation.

Both of them sighed and leaned into his touches.

This was going to be fun. Quinn could already tell that some of their awkwardness and hesitation in their physical relationship came from the fact that they had very similar dispositions. They needed one definite leader, but they were both pleasers—followers, when it came to pursuing pleasure.

He was happy to fill that role for them.

Instead of choosing one or the other to claim first, he urged them together so they could share the moment and loosen up some more. This was about them, not him.

"Kiss each other again. It looked incredible. Better than porn." Because X-rated movies, like a lot of his previous liaisons, weren't about emotion so much as physical intensity. What Trevon and Devra had ran so much deeper than momentary desire.

Quinn shifted his grip so he could rub his thumbs over their lips. Maybe he could experience what that felt like through them because he was as new to this aspect as Devra was to sex itself. An emotional virgin. He was curious and somewhat nervous all at once.

Trevon parted his lips on a low groan while Devra pursed hers and tried to wrap them around Quinn's finger. Not yet.

Quinn wasn't going to budge on that. They were the focus of this exchange. It would stay that way or he wouldn't play along. He wasn't a pawn to be used in their game. He was going to be the one making the rules. And this was one of them—Devra and Trevon came first. His enjoyment and involvement was secondary.

He refused to become a wedge between them.

The husband and wife paused, staring at each other from a few scant inches apart. It seemed insane that they'd done so much to stay together and couldn't get over those final speed bumps keeping them separated. So Quinn nudged them. Literally.

He cupped the backs of their heads and pressed gently but insistently until their mouths made glancing contact. Which was all it took. Devra made a sound—a cross between a whimper and a moan. It turned Quinn's cock to steel in an instant. Trevon was right there to absorb it. He echoed it with a low groan of his own.

Why the hell had these two forced themselves to abstain from enjoying their partner? They were clearly meant for this. For each other. How couldn't they see it?

The moment they connected, they committed to the exploration. Devra went up onto her tiptoes so she could seal their mouths more completely while Trevon speared the fingers of his free hand into her thick, glossy hair. They trembled as he cupped her head.

"Go on. Deeper," Quinn urged Trevon. "Taste her. Put your tongue in her mouth and kiss her like she's your goddamn wife. Yours as much as you are hers."

Spurred on, Trevon grew bolder and more aggressive. His tongue flicked out and pressed into Devra's mouth, making her shiver.

Quinn admired the picture they made. Trevon dark and tall, lean muscles clenched as he held himself in check. Devra, petite yet fierce, fiery and alluring, reacting so naturally to her husband's unleashed passion.

They were going to set the sheets on fire tonight.

Quinn would settle for absorbing even a few degrees of the warmth they generated.

He let them distract each other as he guided them across the wood floor to his bedroom and then inside.

They made out, ravenous now that they'd gotten a taste of what was to come.

Quinn steered them closer to the edge of the bed. He sank to his knees in front of the couple, wishing he could bury his face between each of their legs, taking turns driving them wild as they enjoyed each other.

First, he had to get them naked. Bared to each other and to him. To the truth that was evident to him in this moment.

Devra and Trevon were in love *and* in lust. They simply hadn't given themselves permission to admit it before. It would be a crime to let them waste any more time being together and yet so alone.

It had to be heartbreaking. Soul crushing.

Quinn got to work. He unbuckled Trevon's belt, then pulled open the button at the top of his jeans. By the time he was tugging down the guy's zipper, Trevon was pressing forward, rubbing his stiff cock on Quinn's hands. He was desperate for contact. For acceptance.

Quinn wasn't about to deny him either.

He pushed Trevon's jeans the rest of the way down, shoving them off as Trevon marched in place, helping Quinn remove one of the last barriers between him and his wife and the paradise they were about to discover together that night. His underwear was stripped from his long, powerful legs next. Unceremoniously, Quinn got rid of them, leaving Trevon in his tight black T-shirt before turning to Devra.

Considering she'd never done this before, she seemed to be catching on quickly. She was wild, arching in her husband's grip. One of her feet left the floor as her leg climbed to Trevon's hip, her knee bent around him to pull him closer.

Quinn chuckled. "Not so fast, Devra. Soon. But not yet."

He took her knee in his hands, loving how different she was than Trevon, how petite and yet strong. More assertive. Quinn caressed her thigh and calf until she let him manipulate her, trusting him to take care of her. Of them.

Quinn felt honored that they'd let him in to this place in their relationship. He kissed Devra's hip, then let his fingers wander upward to the waistband of the plum-colored leggings she had on under her sundress. A gasp followed when his fingers snuck inside, against the soft, bare skin of her stomach, then lower to the sensitive place above her mound.

Her legs quivered. So he wrapped his arm around her to keep her steady both for Trevon's continued devouring and his own efforts. It took longer than he wanted to peel the stretchy material from her without ripping it or tugging her off balance. But when he slipped her leggings along with the pale pink cotton panties she'd had on beneath them from her feet, he smiled. She curled her toes in the plush area rug he'd placed under the bed, proving how much she relished every nerve in her body being fired.

Devra was reactive, sensual, and so open to the sensations bombarding her that she felt them down to the pretty pink-painted tips of her toes. This was going to be awesome.

With his playmates naked from the waist down, Quinn rose. He apologized for separating them for the moment it took to rid Devra of her dress. Trevon took care of his own shirt in the meantime, unwilling to wait a single second more than he had to before returning to pleasuring his wife.

In fact, he seemed to have overcome some of his anxieties about Devra's willingness to participate. Maybe they didn't need Quinn after all.

"You two are doing great. You're ready for this. Are you sure you want me to stay?" he rasped, wishing he didn't have to ask. But it was the right thing to do. They deserved to make this decision and to be selfish with their special moment if they thought it was for the best.

"Yes!" Devra cried even as Trevon roared, "Don't go!"

Each of them flung out a hand, searching for him.

Devra whispered, "Show me what to do to make it good for him. Please."

Trevon bared himself on a much deeper level than his naked body. "Make sure I don't get too carried away and hurt her or miss any signs of her changing her mind as we go. I'm already getting lost in how she makes me feel."

Quinn nodded, afraid his eyes might shimmer a little in the indirect lighting, giving away exactly how much their faith meant to him. So much more than a quick romp or a taboo way to get off. It felt...sacred, to be invited into their embrace.

And yet, part of him felt like an intruder. An outsider.

Like always.

He brushed those negative thoughts away and focused on pursuing ecstasy. Pure pleasure radiated off Devra and Trevon in waves powerful enough to saturate him with the feeling, too. Trevon was completely bared now. His cock was the largest Quinn had ever had the pleasure of seeing in person. Thick and long, with heavy balls to match. He would be a lot to handle for anyone, never mind someone with Devra's nonexistent history.

She was so brave to open herself like this to new experiences and foreign beliefs about sex and love. Quinn admired her courage and open-mindedness.

She stood before them with only a basic nude bra on. And yet she seemed so powerful. She had no idea that she held both of the men in the palm of her hand.

Quinn reached around her to unhook the undergarment and peel it down her arms, revealing her breasts to the night air and the pair of very aroused males prepared to worship every inch of her.

They weren't huge. The pert mounds would be perfect to fill his mouth, though. Quinn took Trevon's hand in his and guided it to his wife's chest.

When they were less than an inch from her tight nipples, he hesitated, peering into Devra's eyes and waiting for her tiny nod before filling Trevon's palm with her warm flesh. He squeezed his fingers on top of Trevon's.

All three of them moaned.

Quinn let them discover this new pleasure while he quickly rid himself of his own clothes, throwing them somewhere in the corner of the room, instantly forgotten.

His cock throbbed, so he took it in hand and rubbed it, just enough to soothe the ache there as he watched Devra grind up against Trevon with sultry motions that were better suited to a professional exotic dancer than a woman about to lose her virginity.

"Why don't you lay down? Get more comfortable?" Quinn directed.

He took Devra's shoulders and guided her backward. Trevon followed, refusing to break contact as he kissed his wife over and over. Quinn didn't blame him one bit. If he'd been given an open invitation like that, he'd take full advantage, too.

When they hit the fluffy bedding, Quinn rolled them so that Devra was on her back and Trevon on his side, angled inward. He and Devra were still making out while leaving their bodies open to Quinn's whims.

The better to eat you, my dears, he thought to himself with a wicked smirk.

He spread Devra out on the bed so that both he and Trevon could shower her with bliss. He pushed her ankles apart, then wormed between them. Though he could have reached up and cupped one of her perky breasts, Quinn left that to Trevon.

He wrapped his fingers around Trevon's wrist, watching the guy's cock jerk in response to his touch. *Focus*, he reminded himself. *Take it slow. Introduce them to each other. It's about them, not you.*

So he guided Trevon's hand across his wife's chest, using it to brush over her ruched nipples. On top of Trevon's fingers, he pressed gently, wishing he knew what Devra's skin felt like against Trevon's palm. From Trevon's groan, it was as velvety and smooth as it looked.

Trevon concentrated on Devra's mouth and breasts, whispering reassurances to her between torturously slow kisses. Satisfied, Quinn retreated, allowing Trevon to take over those tasks so he could move on to other, next-level ministrations.

But first he stroked himself a few more times as he watched them explore and play, absorbing their wonder and unadulterated joy. When that didn't suffice any longer, he began to supplement Devra's pleasure, getting her as ready as possible for what would come by beginning at her toes, massaging and kissing his way toward the tops of her legs.

Quinn went as slowly as he could. Nearly impossible for a man used to speeding.

By the time he was close enough to breathe in the scent of her arousal, he thought he might come from the friction of his erection against the sheets alone. His hips ground into them as he rubbed his face against Devra's inner thigh.

She moaned and arched toward him. Although she hadn't experienced this before, her body knew what to do. It reacted to him and Trevon like it was made for them. Or at least for her husband.

Quinn chased away those thoughts by giving Devra more pleasure. He looked up at Trevon, who was watching him with rapt attention.

Trevon nodded. "Go ahead. I want her to be as wet as possible before..."

He didn't say it, but all three of them knew what he meant—before he stretched his wife's unused pussy around his fat cock and fucked her for the first time. Trevon was so concerned about others that her comfort and the quality of her experience mattered more than anything to him, including his own enjoyment.

Quinn thought the guy deserved to be rewarded for that generosity. So as he licked his lips and lowered his mouth toward Devra's waiting pussy, he also reached out. Simultaneously, he connected with Devra's wet flesh and wrapped his hand around Trevon's long, thick cock.

They both cried out his name.

He froze. This wasn't supposed to be about him.

18

Fortunately, Trevon smoothed over Quinn's gaff. He kissed Devra then, staring into her eyes as Quinn prepared her to take her first—and maybe only—lover. Trevon told her over and over how well she was doing, and how beautiful she looked as desire flushed her cheeks and made her eyes wild with passion.

Meanwhile, Trevon's cock jerked in Quinn's hand. It stiffened, growing even more as Quinn began to measure its length with slow, steady pumps of his fist.

Quinn felt like he'd reached the pinnacle of his life. He had the best of both worlds at his fingertips, Devra's softness and Trevon's hardness. They were equally appealing. He buried his face against Devra's core, licking every bit of her that he could reach, paying special attention to her clit with the barest of contact at first, letting her get used to the intensity of the sensation.

And when she reached down and gripped his hair, fisting it in her petite hand, he nearly lost it. The tug on his scalp and the hints of pain only spurred him on.

Quinn ate her, using his tongue to press inside her the barest bit before suckling on her clit.

"Oh, *oh*!" She squirmed and tried to warn them of her impeding explosion but it seemed like she couldn't find the words. It didn't matter. Both Trevon and Quinn understood what her body was telling them.

Trevon wrapped his arm around her and drew her as close to his heaving chest as he could. "I promise I'll keep you safe tonight too. Surrender to it, Devra. I've got you."

Quinn felt his eyes stinging even as he redoubled his efforts.

It was by far the most beautiful thing he'd ever seen, ever been involved in, when she unraveled and came in Trevon's arms, and on Quinn's face. All of her nervousness and trepidation vanished as she rode out the pulses of rapture.

Trevon jerked then, his ass clenched tight, and he looked down at Quinn. "Stop, please. Or I'll be next. Too soon."

With a sigh of regret, Quinn relinquished his hold on Trevon's cock. When Devra realized the men had stopped enjoying themselves and focused on her instead, she shook her head. "No, keep going. I need a minute over here."

Quinn and Trevon exchanged questioning glances.

"I don't know if that's a good idea," Trevon whispered. "I'm so turned on by you and the thought of finally making love to you that I might not be able to prevent myself from coming."

He was so patient and gentle while educating her. It made Quinn's heart beat even faster.

"I understand." She kissed Trevon gently with

lingering brushes of her lips. "But I want to see him taste you, too."

"Why?" he asked.

Devra blushed. "I feel...weak, being this uninhibited and out of control by myself. Naked. It doesn't feel normal."

Quinn stepped in before they could go off the rails again like they had for so long. They thought far too much and needed to feel instead. "I promise you, nothing about this is ordinary and that's a great thing."

She winged her stare to him, her eyes wide and liquid.

Trevon seemed like he was about to object before Quinn silenced him by saying, "The connection you two have is special. But there's nothing debauched or wrong about it. It's...perfection."

Devra relaxed then, basking in the afterglow of her orgasm. Fortunately, Quinn was capable of granting her wish while building her back up at the same time.

"I've got this," he promised Trevon. "I won't let you lose it before you're inside her. She's right, she needs a minute to ramp up again. I'll keep you hard until she's ready."

"That's not going to be a problem." Trevon nuzzled his nose against Devra's, melting part of Quinn's heart.

He couldn't stop himself then. He strained his neck forward and extended his tongue, lapping at the dot of precome on Trevon's tip. It complemented the musk of Devra's arousal left on his taste buds. But that single drop wasn't going to be enough to satisfy his hunger.

Devra surprised them both by reaching down and putting her hand around Trevon's cock, at least as much as she could grip, and aiming it at Quinn's mouth. He didn't hesitate, and plunged Trevon's hard-on deep into his face with one long, fluid stroke. He sucked, licked, and bobbed, taking as much as he could without choking.

Meanwhile, he searched blindly with his left hand until it landed at the juncture of Devra's thighs. He petted her gently, lightly, until her breath came in pants. Only then did his finger swirl around her clit from time to time. And when she finally whimpered, he slid his middle finger down her cleft and began to press against her opening.

Trevon groaned. A spurt of fluid landed on Quinn's tongue, so he pulled off, switching to sucking on the guy's ball sac instead. Trevon's dick slid across Quinn's face while Quinn began to finger Devra with slow, steady penetrations.

Some small part of him rejoiced, knowing he was the first to touch her there, like this.

She was soaking wet and steamy inside. Trevon was going to love burying himself in her sweet, tight pussy. Quinn rocked against the mattress, careful not to over-stimulate himself and break his concentration.

After he'd worked a second and then third finger inside Devra and scissored them open, he recaptured Trevon's cock for a few farewell sucks.

When he lifted his head, he looked up at the couple and said, "It's time. Are you both ready?"

They both nearly shouted, "Yes!" in unison.

So Quinn told them where he wanted them. "Devra, I think this will be best—most comfortable and enjoyable for you—if you get on your hands and knees. I can lay under you to support you and lick your clit while Trevon enters you from behind. He'll have a lot of control that way, and if it's too much for you, all you have to do is lunge forward. Okay?"

"Yes. Fine. Just...hurry." Devra rolled and Quinn helped her into place, then went to his back between their legs and slid up the bed as if he was rolling under a car lift. He had a front-row seat to her deflowering when Trevon straddled them both and aligned the tip of his cock with her pussy.

Trevon leaned over her back and murmured in her ear, "I love you, Devra. Thank you for giving me this part of you."

She turned her head to the side and kissed him before whispering, "It was always yours, Trevon. I just didn't know if you wanted to take it."

"I do. Too badly." He groaned, then rocked the barest bit forward. Not enough to breach her opening, but enough to put pressure there. From his angle, Quinn saw Devra's pussy clench involuntarily in response.

This was the moment they became lovers in addition to soul mates. It was the most beautiful thing he'd ever seen in his life. And the hottest.

Trevon gripped Quinn's bent knee hard enough to get his attention. "Don't let me get carried away and hurt her. Please. Make sure it's good for her, too. I want her to come all over my cock."

They both knew it was going to be heaven for Trevon.

Quinn nodded. "I've got you both. I promise."

Only then did Trevon relent. He released Quinn's knee and blanketed Devra's back, sheltering her with his much larger form. "I've been dreaming of this for so long."

"I wish you would have said so." Devra tipped her head and kissed her husband again and again. "I wish I would have told you that I've been dreaming of it, too. I never thought I could be this lucky."

Quinn held his breath. He felt for the first time like he

was intruding, and peered at the door. He must have shifted in that direction, too.

Trevon noticed and said, "Please don't leave. I need you. Help me."

How could Quinn resist a request like that? He put one hand on Devra's tiny waist to hold her still, then reached beneath her to where Trevon's remarkable cock was poised to enter her body. Beyond ready to be buried deep inside his wife.

Quinn lifted his head off the bed and licked Devra's clit, distracting her and ramping her up again as he tugged Trevon closer by the dick. He fit the fat head of his cock tighter to Devra, who arched her back and dropped even lower, widening her legs so that Trevon could easily invade her tight opening.

Trevon advanced and Devra pushed back, inviting him deeper.

She was a natural. Instincts served her well.

Quinn rubbed the place where Trevon's cock met her core, wetting his shaft with Devra's own slickness. When he wasn't sure if that would be enough, he licked his fingers and added his spit to the natural lubrication easing the insertion of Trevon's cock.

Trevon's thighs quivered, and his balls drew up tighter to his body.

Devra's first time would be memorable as fuck, but it wasn't going to be the sort of lovemaking that would last all night. None of them would survive that.

So Quinn did his best to make sure she enjoyed it more than most women did when they lost their virginity. He suckled her clit with short, soft pulses as Trevon advanced then retreated before returning a little farther on each stroke. He worked his cock inside his wife until she held him fully within her, a feat Quinn hadn't really thought possible.

Her pussy was stretched around Trevon's girth, but she didn't seem to mind.

No, she ground herself on Quinn's face, riding him as surely as she did Trevon's cock.

Both men moaned and gave her every bit of enjoyment they could. Quinn reached up with one hand and pinched her nipple, making her squirm and rock faster against them.

Time after time, she moaned Trevon's name and once or twice Quinn's. She lost all semblance of her usual propriety and gave herself over entirely to the flood of emotions and sensations they created together.

Her lower abdomen clenched once and then a couple more times in front of Quinn's face as she fought her climax. The end was nearing.

So Quinn cupped Trevon's balls in his hand and used the grip to pull the man forward. No matter how hesitant he was, he wasn't about to resist Quinn's hold there. He groaned and shouted first Devra's name, and then Quinn's. His nuts tightened in Quinn's palm.

Oh hell no, he wasn't going to cut Devra's experience short. No way. He had to last a little bit longer, until she'd shattered around Trevon's fully embedded cock. Nothing else would suffice in Quinn's mind.

So he squeezed, the barest bit, making Trevon yelp, then relax. He murmured, "Thanks, man."

Devra looked over her shoulder and Trevon put his hand lightly on her neck before kissing her again. That drove his cock inside her as he leaned forward for better contact.

One thrust lodged him to the limit in Devra's pussy,

causing her to gasp and freeze. Quinn immediately put his hand on Trevon's thigh and kept him from proceeding.

The other guy made a confused sound as he wondered why he couldn't keep drilling forward, pursuing the most enjoyable sex of his life. Until he realized what had happened.

"Oh shit. I'm sorry." He hugged Devra to his chest, soothing her by kissing the crook of her neck and cradling her until the pain of his advance subsided.

"I'm all right now. Just needed a second." She sighed and melted into Trevon's arms. "Keep going, please. I'm almost there."

Quinn smiled and rewarded her frankness with a kiss over her clit followed by his tongue tracing circles around it. It wasn't long before she was moaning and rocking backward again, facilitating Trevon's glides in and out of her tight sheath.

This time they were peaking in unison.

Quinn applied more pressure to Devra's clit and breast. And with his other hand, he reached beyond Trevon's balls, hoping Devra's arousal was enough to make his spontaneous maneuver a success.

Trevon was riding Devra with measured thrusts that rocked the entire bed. She was meeting him stroke for stroke. And then she screamed, beating her fists on the pillow. Her pussy spasmed and wrung Trevon's cock.

That's when Quinn slipped his finger in Trevon's ass.

The guy shouted. His balls clenched rhythmically as he joined his wife in a powerful orgasm. The climax caused him to hug Quinn's finger. The couple shuddered and bucked together, never once slipping apart. Quinn kept up his motions, sucking, probing, and rubbing until they both seemed ready to collapse and he was in danger of being crushed.

Only then did Trevon withdraw his spent cock from Devra's pussy. A pearlescent stream of his ejaculate decorated her swollen flesh. Quinn figured he deserved the prize and licked it from her as gently as possible, triggering aftershocks that had her pressing her pussy against his face a few final times.

When Trevon crashed to the bed and gathered Devra to his chest, she went willingly into his embrace.

"Thank you, thank you," she whispered in between kisses on his collarbone. "I love you so much. I couldn't have imagined a better experience for my first time. Thank you for giving me this night."

Seeing that he'd done what he set out to do, Quinn felt his own cock jerk.

Without even touching himself, he came hard enough to launch jet after jet of come from his balls all over his chest. He wondered if they would even notice, lost in their revelations about love, sex, and each other.

Of course they did.

Devra pouted, and Trevon said, "Sorry. I was going to help you with that."

"Nah. I'm good." Quinn flashed them a crooked smile. If it didn't quite reach to his heart, that was his problem. He'd known what he was signing up for and he'd achieved his goal. He'd helped them come together and that was the best reward he could have asked for. "In fact, why don't you two take my bed? I'll sleep over at your place."

Devra and Trevon exchanged worried glances, but that was exactly what he didn't want—to disrupt the progress they'd made. So he rolled from his bed and stood by the side of it looking down at the two people he was sure he'd never forget in all his life.

He bent over and stole one tiny kiss from Devra and then paused before doing the same with Trevon. The guy groaned and raised his shoulders from the bed as if he wanted a hell of a lot more than that chaste peck, but Quinn wasn't offering.

Not tonight and probably not ever.

This had been penance, not something to enjoy, although he had anyway.

"Thank you," Devra whispered, and Trevon nodded his agreement.

"Goodnight." Although it threatened to rip his soul in half, Quinn forced himself to put one foot in front of the other and leave the happy couple behind.

He started to cross the yard but knew he wouldn't be able to bring himself to go inside. It wasn't like he was going to fall asleep anytime soon anyway. So he settled for lying down in the grass and studying the stars, wondering where in the universe he fit in.

Was there a soul mate out there for him?

Would he ever find him or her or them?

Could they be any more perfect for him than Devra and Trevon, who weren't his to keep?

He didn't think so.

19

Devra took a deep, if shaky, breath. *You can do this,* she coached herself repeatedly before resolving to be as kind, yet honest, as she could be. Her future happiness—Trevon's, and maybe Quinn's, too—depended on this talk going well. It had been nearly a week of strained smiles and frantic lovemaking with her husband followed by silence as they lay awake, neither able to sleep. No matter how much they fucked, it didn't seem to satisfy either of them the way it had that first time.

They were stuck in limbo. In some bizarre gray area. If they didn't resolve this soon, they would break. She refused to allow that after how hard they'd fought to get here.

Devra walked into the kitchen and sat down at the two-person table across from Trevon, who looked like he'd hardly dozed off again the night before. His lids drooped and he clung to his coffee mug like a lifeline.

"Trevon..."

"I know. We have to talk about this." He lifted his gaze

to hers. The warmth of his rich brown eyes seemed dampened by the bloodshot whites surrounding them.

"We do." She reached out and put her hand over his. "Because I love you. I need you to understand that."

"I love you, too." He lifted her fingers to his lips and kissed them. "I know you don't always believe that we would be together if circumstances were different, but I'm so glad to have you in my life. You're my best friend and now...more."

"We owe Quinn for that." She smiled softly, hoping what she was about to say didn't change how he felt about her.

"We do." He nodded. "But that night..."

"It changed everything," Devra blurted.

"For me, too." Trevon scrunched his eyes closed then said quietly. "I want more. Of you. And him, too. Shit, I'm greedy as fuck. But..."

"Hey, it's okay." Devra steeled herself to be as fearless as he had always been and admit the truth. "I still want him, too. And I sort of want to see where things go. Between all of us, individually and maybe together. You're right, you know? I do feel guilty about tying you down. I know this isn't what you would have chosen for yourself."

"That doesn't mean I don't want to be where I am now." He stiffened, as if daring her to argue that point.

"I'm trying to believe that. But it would help me to accept it as truth if...maybe..." The words got stuck in her throat. It was so wild. Would he think she'd lost her mind? Or maybe that she was a total whore?

"Go ahead, Devra. We don't have any secrets and we shouldn't start keeping them now. If you can picture a way out of this, one that could end in us being happy for the long term, I want to know about it. Because I can't see it. I don't see any way for this mess we've gotten ourselves in to end up in anything but disaster." He paused then whispered, "I'm afraid."

"Of what?" She tipped her head. Was he scared of exploring the part of him that enjoyed men? She knew his family would never have approved. But they were gone now. And she did. She'd support him no matter how this turned out.

"I don't want to risk losing you. You're an incredible person. The past few days have been...great." He cursed under his breath. "That should be enough."

"But it's obviously not." She cleared her throat. "For me either. Okay?"

His eyes widened. "Are you sure?"

Devra nodded. "I can't stop thinking about the fact that we didn't really sleep with him. That we let him leave like that..."

"The look in his eyes..." Trevon downed half his mug, but it wasn't going to help. "It's been torture at work. He's not the same. We cut him."

"I know. Shit, Trevon. I think we really screwed up." Now that it was out there between them, it was like a flood of emotion and explanations burst from inside her. "I want to see what it's like between him and me, and I want you to sleep with him. I want you to come back to me...if you decide that's what you want...and be sure that I'm the person you want most. Or, if not, that you are as happy as you can possibly be. You deserve that."

"And so do you." Trevon nodded. "It goes both ways, you know? Sometimes I'm afraid you're with me because I was the only option you had and now you feel indebted. It fucks me up sometimes. I can't...do all the things I want with you knowing that you might not believe you have other options even now. Besides, you've only ever slept with me, and that's new, too. You should at least try someone else so you can be sure I'm what you want."

Seriously? He thought...

Damn, they were more damaged than she'd realized.

"I will always choose you." She smiled. "But I think we should experiment. For both our sakes."

Trevon smiled back. "I only have one question."

"Yeah? What's that?" An answering grin spread across her face.

"Will you be there when I sleep with him? I want you to see it for yourself. To make your own informed decisions. I don't want to do this in isolation or behind your back. That seems counter to everything we're committing to going forward." Trevon locked eyes with her. "I want this to work."

Devra really thought about the ramifications before she responded. There would be no hiding their true feelings if they were all in it together. That was what they should do. "Okay. And same goes. You'll be there when I sleep with him so you can see for yourself that you're meant for me and would have been no matter how I met you. Except..."

Trevon nudged his foot against hers under the table. "Don't chicken out now—what?"

"I liked how he took control. It seems like you and I have floundered around without direction. Maybe that's what we need. Someone who likes to be in charge to prod us when we get bogged down by our thoughts and insecurities. Someone who doesn't let us wander in circles for years. Someone who pushes us to be the best versions of ourselves and refuses to let our relationship get stale."

"Something about it definitely worked." Trevon shrugged. "I want to do it again. Soon."

"Me, too." Relief inspired a grin to spread slowly over her lips. For the first time in days, she felt like she could breathe again.

"So...who's going to come on to him first?"

"Rock, paper, scissors, best two out of three," Devra proposed.

"Fair enough, Mrs. Russell."

She knew she should have been bummed when Trevon's scissors cut her paper, but exhilaration raced through her instead. Watching her husband with Quinn might be even sexier than sleeping with him herself.

20

Devra was nervous.

Not for herself, but for her husband.

They'd discussed the best way to go about getting what they wanted, and what she was pretty sure Quinn needed. In the end, they'd decided to be spontaneous. Trevon kept toying with the hem of his shirt, shifting restlessly as he did when he was anxious, though she couldn't say if it was because he was looking for the right opening to make his proposition, or because he was terrified of being rejected.

Either way, she'd be there to support him.

They were hanging out at Quinn's house, as they did almost every night lately. Since his kitchen was larger than theirs, she was tinkering with a new recipe, occasionally asking the guys to taste her creations and give feedback. They loved everything she made, though, so it was more fun than helpful to feed them.

Instead of watching a movie, the guys had decided to play video games. Devra was a little surprised. Trevon had never expressed interest in that since she'd known him.

Maybe because they didn't have extra cash for a gaming system, but he'd never even mentioned it. He preferred to be doing things outside—working with his hands, not playing with them. Maybe he was humoring Quinn since the other guy had suggested it and said it wasn't any fun playing by himself.

"Want to wager on it?" Trevon asked, perking Devra's ears up.

They didn't have anything to gamble. Except maybe themselves.

Quinn grinned. "I'm always up for a bet. What are the stakes?"

"Loser gives the winner a blowjob."

Devra dropped a baking sheet of baklava onto the granite countertop with a clatter. American bluntness still caught her off guard sometimes.

Both men whipped around to look at her. Shit, she'd ruined Trevon's chance.

"You okay?" Trevon asked.

Devra nodded. Okay? She was about to spontaneously combust. It might not have been right or proper, but thinking of watching Quinn give Trevon as much pleasure as her husband had been giving her these past several days...it turned her on as high as the oven.

Quinn looked between her and her husband. His eyes narrowed. "Why do I feel like I'm being set up?"

"It wasn't a trick question. But yes, Devra and I discussed the possibility of...you and me. Doing stuff." Trevon shrugged. "There are things we still need to figure out between us, and one of them is the fact that—"

He stumbled over how to put it politely.

So Devra imagined how Mustang Sally would act in this situation, and said what Trevon couldn't. "I found out what it was like to have sex with a man last week. Trevon still hasn't had that opportunity. He needs to before we can decide where we go from here."

Quinn rubbed his jaw. What was he thinking?

Hopefully he realized that not just any man off the street would suffice for this experiment. It was about him, too. They had a connection with him. Almost like he really understood their struggles and what it had taken to get to even this precarious point in their relationship and in life.

"Fuck the game then. You don't have to concoct some elaborate scheme to get in my pants. If that's what you want, ask." Quinn stared at Trevon.

"Can I suck your cock?"

"Jesus, Trevon. I'm not a good enough man to say no to that." Quinn's jaw tightened. "You can have me any fucking time you want."

Trevon looked to Devra, who nodded. This was what he'd been hoping for and dreaming of for a while now. She wasn't about to stop him before he got what he needed.

"Now. I want you right now." Trevon angled himself toward the other guy.

Quinn sat, relaxed, his arms spread behind him across the top of his sofa. His knees were set wide apart and his socked feet planted in the surprisingly soft midnight blue rug. "Don't worry, Trevon. Just the idea of you going down on me is so incredible that I'm not going to last long. You're going to get off easy."

Trevon laughed, some of the tension in the room evaporating with their banter. "No, you've got it backwards. *You're* going to get off easy."

"You don't think I'm the kind of guy to take without

173

reciprocating, do you?" Quinn's teasing tone faltered. Didn't he realize they thought the world of him?

He'd done nothing but shower them with kindness, acceptance, and the sparks of arousal and attraction that had goaded them into taking a leap of faith they'd been too scared to make on their own.

"What if I don't want a blowjob from you?" Trevon murmured, staring at the ground.

Quinn flinched until he realized Trevon hadn't meant it like it had sounded. He put his hand under Trevon's chin and lifted it until they met eye to eye. Once he detected the same uncertainty and desperation Devra did in Trevon's walnut eyes—even darker now that he was aroused and even a little scared—Quinn relaxed. "Then I'll give you whatever it is you do want."

"Your cock," Trevon said plainly, making Devra shiver.

"Where?" Quinn wondered, probably not because he wasn't sure but because he wanted Trevon to admit it. To own his desires. To accept them and Quinn.

Devra would have hugged them both if she wasn't too afraid of interrupting the moment. They were so perfect and so damaged in their own ways. Ways that made her feel like she wasn't such a failure for her own issues. They might not agree, and would likely consider their emotions weaknesses, but they made her adore them both even more.

"Inside me. My ass." Trevon swallowed. "Please."

Quinn nodded slowly. Then, while still staring into Trevon's eyes, he unbuckled his black leather and chain belt. It rattled in the absolute silence. Devra would remember the sound of it for the rest of her life.

Trevon licked his full lips as he fixated on Quinn's fingers, which unbuttoned his jeans then ripped open the fly. He lifted his hips and ordered Trevon, "Take these off me."

Her husband reached out, his hands stopping barely an inch from Quinn's clothing and the gorgeous body beneath. He looked to her. This was the point of no return and they both knew it.

"Go ahead, Trevon. Do as he says." She wondered if they would object to her sliding her dress up her thighs and touching herself while they entertained each other. Seeing them like this, raw and exposed, aroused her more than she'd expected.

"Why don't you join us?" Quinn asked quietly. "Come sit here and see how incredible your husband makes me feel."

Trevon looked at her and admitted, "It will make me more comfortable if I can see you and know that you aren't disgusted by what we're doing."

That settled it. Devra practically flew to the couch. She sat cross-legged facing the two men. It was easy for them to notice her panties and the wet spot on the crotch of them. Trevon especially had a perfect view of the proof of her approval. "You see that I'm not, right?"

He nodded.

Quinn groaned. He said to Trevon, "She should enjoy the show, right? Touch herself? Make herself come if she likes watching us like this?"

Trevon nodded again, as if speaking was beyond him.

When Quinn switched his attention to Devra, for just a moment, there was no denying him. "Do it, Devra. Whatever feels right as you witness our passion, you should do it."

She blushed. Could he guess that despite her bravado in front of the Hot Rods ladies, she'd never masturbated before? At home, it would have been too dangerous to get caught doing something so wicked. And since she'd met Trevon, well, things had been awkward at first. She'd learned to suppress these parts of herself. These desires. In a way, Quinn and Trevon were freeing her again. Giving her permission to discover herself.

And she would take it.

"Now get back to what you were doing." Quinn lasered his gaze on Trevon, who jerked. He gripped the waistband of Quinn's jeans and dragged it down the man's powerful legs, his knuckles brushing the hairy surface of Quinn's skin as he went.

"My socks, too."

Trevon removed them before returning his attention to Quinn's crotch. Quinn hadn't been wearing underwear, which left his hard-on bare and ready. He leaned forward slightly, put a hand behind his back, fisted the soft cotton covering it, and ripped his shirt off.

Devra fanned her face. His chest was so muscular and covered in ink, which did nothing to detract from his male beauty. Trevon must have thought so, too, because he leaned forward and licked one of Quinn's nipples.

Did men enjoy that?

Quinn cursed and clutched Trevon's skull, pinning her husband's lips to his tightening skin. *Huh.* Guess so. Devra swore she was learning more with every second she spent in their company.

Trevon was noisy as he licked and sucked on Quinn's chest. Both men moaned and Trevon's hips rocked, thrusting into the cushion of the couch in front of him as he feasted.

"That's right," Quinn crooned. He ran his hands over

Trevon's head, neck, and shoulders. "You can have me. Take whatever you need."

A strangled groan fell from Trevon as he began to work his way lower. Devra knew just how good it felt when he licked, sucked, and nipped a path across her own torso, so she shivered along with Quinn as Trevon did the same to his new lover.

She pressed her hand between her legs in an attempt to hold in the ache forming there. It was no use. So she began to move her fingers in small circles over her underwear while Trevon approached the blunt head of Quinn's cock.

He paused, inspecting Quinn up close, from the drop of fluid in the slit there to the veins standing out in relief on his shaft, and lower to the balls hanging between his thighs. He wasn't nearly as big as Trevon, but that didn't seem to matter to her husband, who licked his lips.

"You going to stare at it all day or play with it?" Quinn asked.

Trevon's nostrils flared. He opened his mouth and took Quinn inside, plunging downward until Quinn's cock was buried deep. Which was when he choked.

Devra put her hand on Trevon's shoulder, as if she could do anything to help.

"Damn, Trevon." Quinn took hold of her husband's face and lifted it a few inches. "Not so fast. Take it easy. Suck me. God, yes. Like that. Now...slowly..."

He guided Trevon's head lower bit by bit until he had time to adjust. His jaw worked as he found a comfortable position and then slid even lower. Quinn's cock had to be pressing into his throat by now.

Then Trevon didn't need any guidance. He licked, sucked, and bobbed over Quinn, making the other guy gasp, curse, and groan. "I can't believe you've only done this once before. You're so fucking good at it."

Trevon seemed to relax a little at that, his hands unfisting where they rested on the couch.

"Play with my balls, too." Quinn spread himself wider, granting Trevon full access.

He took it, rolling Quinn's balls in his palm and squeezing them, a little harder than Devra would have been comfortable doing. She mimicked his motions on herself—rubbing, teasing, and pressing.

It was only a few minutes more before Quinn began to get restless. Devra, too. She slipped her fingers inside the leg band of her panties and pressed one inside herself. She moaned.

Both Trevon and Quinn paused.

"Enough." Quinn levered himself off the couch, dislodging Trevon in the process.

Trevon blinked, as if startled at losing his new favorite treat. But not for long.

"Strip. Quickly." Quinn was so much more forceful with Trevon than he had been with Devra. It was like two completely different sides to his personality. She could see where he needed both, too. The softness and the hardness. The ability to be defenseless warring with the need to be in control.

It was fascinating and incredibly enlightening to see the two men interact like this.

Trevon seemed grateful that for once he didn't have to be in charge. He could relax and obey. His trust in Quinn meant he could let go and be sure everything would be taken care of.

They were a perfect match.

So where did that leave Devra? She nibbled on her

lower lip as Trevon got undressed. Fully naked, he was so stunning. Made entirely of grace and power and empathy.

Quinn clearly appreciated the sight, too. He stroked his cock, still slick with Trevon's spit, and walked a circle around her husband. The fingers of his other hand trailed across Trevon's collarbones then down his back and over the swell of his tight ass. "Damn, Trevon."

Devra completely agreed. Damn indeed.

"Turn around. Get on your hands and knees." Quinn pressed Trevon's shoulders until he did as he was told, sinking to the open space on the carpet and waiting for Quinn to join him.

Quinn looked to Devra, then jerked his chin toward his bedroom. "Would you go in there? In the top drawer of the dresser, there's a bottle of lube. Bring it to me, please."

"Of course." Devra wasn't afraid to admit she liked it when he bossed her around, even though he did it nicely. He had something that she and Trevon were missing. An ability to make things happen. To get things done. To bring them all together and take what they needed even if they were afraid to.

She dashed into the other room and back as fast as possible, clutching the plastic container of clear liquid. When she handed it to him, he smiled as if he were a perfect gentleman, although they knew—in the best possible way—that was far from the truth. "Thank you."

"You're welcome." She couldn't say what came over her then, but she said, "Only the best for my husband."

Devra hoped Quinn realized that she was talking about him.

He nodded as if he took the responsibility seriously. Then he pointed. "If you don't mind, go sit by his head so you can see his face when I fuck his tight ass. Tell me if he needs a break."

"I will." Just like Quinn had been there when Trevon had taken her for the first time and made sure it was so damn good for her, now she could return the favor.

"Devra?" Quinn said as she began to lower herself to the floor near her husband.

"Yes?"

"You're overdressed. Feel free to get more comfortable." Quinn studied her modest floral dress as if it was some sexy runway couture. She'd be lying if she said she hadn't wanted to get rid of it and her underwear anyway.

Devra peeled her clothes off bit by bit, hoping her reserve came off more as seduction.

"You're so damn beautiful, Devra," Trevon whispered reverently. "It means everything to me that you're here and that you support me. This. You're so fucking brave to let me try it and to do it with me."

Meanwhile, Quinn poured some of the gel on his hands and began to rub them together, warming the slick substance.

By the time Devra settled in front of Trevon—as he began to kiss her knee and then her thigh, in between whispered thanks—Quinn was ready to return his full attention to her husband.

He slipped his hand between Trevon's legs, teasing his cock and then balls before moving upward. He spread slickness over Trevon's hole before working the tip of one finger into the opening.

"Fuck." Trevon held her hand so tight, she thought he might leave a dent.

"Does it feel good?" she asked softly, rubbing his head with her other hand.

"Yes." He leaned into her caress.

"Did he tell you that I did this the other day when he came inside you?" Quinn asked, making Devra gasp. "I could feel his whole body quaking as he shot so hard, deep in your pussy."

Trevon looked up at her guiltily.

"I'm glad you liked it as much as I did." The reminder of that moment, the first time they'd been joined, filled her with joy. She didn't want it to be one of the few times they did it either. If this was what it took, how she had to accept him in order to keep even a piece of him for herself, she would gladly share him. Even part of Trevon was plenty to make her happy.

Devra put her fingers over Trevon's where they were clutched in the carpet. "This is all about you. Don't worry about anything else. Enjoy what he's giving you."

"And what your wife is giving you, too. This is all because of her," Quinn said as he added a second finger, stretching Trevon. Even two digits were slight compared to his cock, but Devra had to trust that he knew what he was doing and that he would make himself fit without hurting Trevon.

"I know. I love you, Devra," Trevon swore.

"I love you, too." She kissed him and he trembled.

Quinn had removed his fingers and was filling his hand with more lubrication. "Ready?" he asked Trevon as he transferred it to his own flesh with long, hard strokes of his fist over the steely flesh.

"I've been ready. For so long." Trevon looked up at Devra and she smiled, brushing her finger over his swollen lips. She couldn't resist leaning forward to kiss him again, tenderly. And that's when Quinn advanced.

Trevon froze, then groaned.

When she lifted her head so she could study his expression, the tip of Quinn's cock was already embedded in Trevon's ass. Her husband had his eyes closed, but he was pressing his body backward, welcoming the invasion.

Devra didn't care anymore about propriety. She spread her legs on either side of Trevon's strong arms and began to rub her pussy as Quinn speared Trevon on his dick. All the while, he spoke softly to Trevon, telling him how good it felt to be inside him and how courageous he was to finally experience what he'd dreamed of for so long.

Quinn rubbed his hands down Trevon's back, helping him relax. So Devra did the same, massaging his shoulders and telling him how damn sexy he looked on the end of Quinn's dick.

When Quinn was fully sheathed in her husband's body, he looked at her and grinned. "He was made for this."

He was. But was he made for Quinn or for Devra?

She wasn't sure.

Trevon looked over his shoulder at Quinn then. He asked, "Can I eat her while you fuck me. Please?"

"That's up to your wife, not me." Quinn smacked Trevon's muscled rear. "But I'd sure as hell love to see that while I'm enjoying your ass. Son of a bitch, you feel so good around me."

Devra didn't hesitate. Her only answer was to tip back using one straight-locked arm for support so she didn't miss any of the show they were putting on for her. Then she arched her spine and presented herself to Trevon.

A strangled groan left his throat as he buried his face

between her legs and began to devour her as if she tasted better than the spicy shakshouka he loved so much.

Quinn turned feral. His hips began to move, thrusting in and out as he leaned forward far enough that he bit Trevon's shoulder. It looked like a wild animal claiming its mate, and that did nothing to keep Devra's passion at bay.

She quivered as Trevon's tongue lapped at her arousal and then upward to her clit.

Devra thought there was a good chance that she'd be the first of the three of them to climax. Witnessing the men take care of each other and their explosive passion was infectious.

Quinn fucked Trevon with increasing speed and power. His hips smacked against Trevon's, which drove her husband's mouth harder against her pussy.

Just when she thought she was going to explode, Quinn smacked Trevon's ass again, hard enough to get his attention. "This is fun, but I want to play with your cock. You're going to come all over yourself while I fuck you. Show me and your wife how much you love my dick."

Trevon moved so fast, Devra nearly fell over. He flipped to his back and stared up at Quinn. "Yes, please. Make me."

"I will. But only if you pleasure your wife first." His brilliant blue eyes cut to her as he said, "Get up. Kneel over him. Let him finish what he started. If he does a good job, I'll give him what he's begging for."

Devra couldn't even form a response to that except to crawl closer. Trevon wrapped his hands around her. His long, dark fingers looked so beautiful against her paler skin where they nearly encircled her waist. He drew her into position and resumed blowing her mind.

Quinn smiled at her and cupped her cheek in his hand. "You're spectacular. In every way."

Before she could thank him and say the same, he fit himself back to Trevon and slid deep inside. He curled his arms around Trevon's thighs and held him in place as he began to fuck in earnest.

And that's when Devra noticed Trevon's massive erection bobbing on his rock-hard abs. Without thinking, she reached for it.

He bucked, nearly dislodging Quinn.

"Don't you dare come. Not until Devra does," Quinn reminded him.

Fortunately for Trevon, that wasn't going to take very long at all. Devra moaned and ground her pussy against Trevon's face, putting his tongue where she liked it.

She only needed one more thing to set her off. And she knew exactly what it was.

Devra reached out and put her free hand on Quinn's shoulder. He must have thought she was balancing herself because he resisted for a moment when she tugged him toward her.

When he finally came closer, she smiled and whispered, "Kiss me."

Their lips collided. It wasn't the smoothest caress of all time given their position, her jerking Trevon's cock, him fucking, and the incredible things Trevon was doing between her legs. But it was enough.

She opened her eyes, looked directly at Quinn, and hoped he could see how much he'd given them. Today, in bed, and in general.

He deserved to be as happy as he'd made them.

While he stared at her with wide, startled eyes, she surrendered.

Devra came on her husband's face, while kissing another man. She felt Trevon's cock jerk in response and gripped him tighter. He groaned and squirmed beneath her and Quinn, obviously joining her in an epic release. She felt his come land hot on her belly as he emptied himself.

And only when they'd both nearly drowned in ecstasy did Quinn follow suit.

He threw his head back and shouted, "Trevon! Devra!"

His motions became frantic and then jerky. He buried himself completely in Trevon then spasmed, mashing their bodies together and filling her husband to overflowing with his seed.

The thought alone made Devra come again.

Her orgasm was so powerful, she lost control of her muscles and collapsed backward on the rug.

Trevon reached blindly for her, his big hand wrapping around her ankle and using the connection to draw her alongside him. He buried his face in the crook of her neck and clutched her to his chest. "Thank you. Thank you. I love you. Thank you."

Devra felt tears sting her eyes as she held him and whispered reassuring nonsense. They lay there cuddled together, recovering. By the time they calmed down enough to look around for Quinn, he was nowhere to be found.

21

Trevon was cleaning up his station during a rare gap in his schedule when a long white van rolled into the lot. The lettering on the side proclaimed it belonged to Dawes Salvage Services.

When the door opened, the guy who popped out was shorter than Trevon—though most people were. He had a scrappy look about him, like you wouldn't want to try to cheat him at cards or pool in a bar or he'd kick your ass despite being wiry and lean. He had long chestnut hair that brushed his shoulders and a proper beard, maybe a little longer than appropriate for an office but not quite hipster qualified either.

He wore a black long-sleeved shirt despite the heat, though the top three silver snaps were undone, exposing a decently hairy chest and a smattering of tattoos. If Trevon hadn't recently become obsessed with Quinn, he might think the guy was pretty sexy in an unconventional sort of way.

"Hey," he called as the salvage man approached,

drawing him toward the open bay door instead of the small office space attached to the garage.

The guy put his hand up like a visor, then peered inside. "Hello? Quinn, that you?"

"He and Gavyn went to deliver a bike." Trevon leaned up against the counter. "They left me holding down the fort."

It meant something to him that they trusted him enough to look after Hot Rides even for a couple of hours.

"I don't think we've met yet." The man came forward with a spring in his step that matched his easy smile. "I'm Oliver Dawes, but most people call me Ollie. I spend most of my days rummaging through garbage to find anything useful. Especially for vehicles."

"Nice to meet you." Trevon looked over at Pop's bike. It was coming along, but they'd hit a few snags, like cams and other parts they couldn't easily repair or fake. If Trevon had been working a couple more months at Hot Rides, he might have use for Ollie's skills.

"Is that yours?" Ollie pointed at the Indian Chief.

"Yeah." Trevon nodded.

"Then I think my package is actually for you." He took a bundle wrapped in brown burlap from his backpack and handed it over to Trevon.

"What's this?" He flipped open the fabric and found a treasure trove of vintage, pristine parts for his motorcycle inside. "What the—?"

"Quinn asked me to be on the lookout for them." The guy grinned. "I think I see why now. Who needs roses when you can have a big, hard cam shaft, huh?"

Trevon tried to laugh off the joke, but it hit a little close to home. So he simply stared. "This is...thank you. But I can't afford these. I saw a shitty one on eBay for $450 last week. I know he meant well, but Quinn probably didn't realize."

"He put it on the Hot Rides account, buddy. They're yours." Ollie held his hands palms out, refusing to take them back when Trevon thrust them at him. "Even if they hadn't been paid for, I'd leave them here. They belong in that motorcycle, not sitting in someone's warehouse waiting for an internet order to come in for top dollar. It's the best thing about my job, really. Bringing things back to life."

"Wow, that's...thank you." Trevon cleared his throat. "Do you only sell parts or whole bikes, too?"

"If I was ever lucky enough to find one like this, I'd hire Quinn to fix it up for me and then flip it. I go to a lot of auctions and estate sales, I see a lot of collectors. Someone would love to snap up something like that." Ollie wandered closer and crouched down for a better look. "Why? You looking to sell?"

Trevon knew it was for the best. It still hurt like hell when he said, "Yes."

"Let me take a few pictures and see who I run into over the next few weeks. It'll probably take you guys that long to finish it, don't you think?" Ollie wondered.

"I can have it ready in two to three, if the price is right. Now that I have these." Trevon held up the spare parts that had just made a lot of things possible for him and Devra.

"It's a '38 Chief, isn't it?"

Impressive. "Yes. That's right."

"What would you ask for it?"

Trevon shot for the moon. "Forty thousand."

"Son of a bitch." Ollie looked up so fast he nearly fell on his ass. "Are you joking?"

189

"Too much?" Trevon considered lowering his asking price although it cracked his heart in half.

"Hell no!" The guy shook his head, sending his hair whipping around his face. "Take nothing less than fifty. I've seen them go for that much in far worse condition and I know the two of you will have this thing pristine."

"You realize you could have bought it off me and made yourself a nice profit." Trevon raised a brow at Ollie.

"If I was a dickhead, which I'm not." He rolled his eyes as he stood and dusted off his pants. "Besides, I have a feeling for that Quinn would have put his boot so far up my ass it would have come out my mouth. He doesn't hire just anyone to work here. In fact, you're the first, huh?"

Trevon tried not to think of Quinn and firsts or he'd definitely give Ollie the wrong impression. "Uh, I guess."

"Well, tell him I said thanks for his business and that if he ever wants to hire someone else, I'm game for working exclusively for Hot Rides and their friends down the road. It seems like lately you guys are my best customers anyway." The guy laughed, but something about his joke seemed serious to Trevon.

"I'll do that. Thank you again. For the parts and for your help with my pop's bike." Trevon petted the seat lovingly. Someone else would appreciate it like he—and his grandfather before him—had.

"Wait, that's an heirloom?" Ollie crossed his arms. "You sure you want to sell?"

Trevon drew a deep breath and thought of his new family. Devra, and maybe Quinn, too. They wouldn't be whole, or able to move forward, until Devra's immigration status was cleared up and they had some capital to work with for pursuing her dreams. "Positive."

"Okay then. I'll give the shop a call if I get any leads." Ollie nodded.

Trevon realized he should have asked earlier... "What's your finder's fee?"

"It's on the house." He shrugged. "A favor for my best customers."

Trevon wasn't an idiot. He knew the guy could sense he was desperate. "No wonder you need a steady job. You kinda suck at this."

Ollie cracked up. "You're probably right. I like you, Trevon. I think you're going to fit in well around here."

Trevon thought Ollie would, too. He was going to talk to Gavyn and Quinn later about the prospects and what had gone down. There might be more opportunity to use salvage as part of their business strategy as they expanded.

"Hey, I've got nothing to do for the next hour. Want a drink? Something to eat? My wife is a phenomenal cook. I think there are some leftover falafels in the fridge." Trevon wasn't sure what made him ask, but maybe it was that glimpse of loneliness he spotted in the guy's expression before he turned to go. Trevon knew it well and could relate.

It didn't cost anything to be kind. Besides, he was pretty short on friends himself.

"You sure that's cool?" Ollie asked, peeking around as if it was a trap and Gavyn and Quinn were about to pop out from behind a toolbox and chase him off.

"Absolutely." They'd be the first people to welcome a drifter.

Trevon knew, because that's what they'd done for him. And they'd changed his entire life with that one simple act.

22

A week or so later, Quinn was wrapping up a project while Trevon had already started working on the Indian. He'd gone to the cottage to grab some design sketches he'd done the night before for the paint job.

Devra was supervising while she read a cooking magazine, making notes on the recipes inside. Every once in a while she answered the phone or fielded questions from walk-ins, not that there were many of those. She even responded to a few email inquiries for him, which he really appreciated since administrative bullshit drove him crazy.

Gavyn was out again. He hadn't even given a reason for his absence this time. For all they knew he was at home, sneaking in some afternoon loving with Amber.

Quinn was starting to wonder if the guy was doing it on purpose, either as some misplaced matchmaking attempt or because he wanted Quinn to know he had things under control on his own.

Either way, the end result was that they had the place to themselves. Again.

And his cock wanted to do something a lot more fun than cleaning the shop or even making more progress on the Indian restoration, which was coming along nicely thanks to the parts Ollie had scrounged from who knew where.

Quinn picked up his largest wrench and started to put it away when he caught Devra peeking at him over the top of her reading material.

"Hey, baby, I've got a really big tool. Want to see?" he teased as he waved the metal in her direction. Stupid, yup. But he was really horny and quickly losing brain cells to blood flow problems.

"Compensating for something?" She rolled her eyes at him.

"You know I'm not, but I'm willing to prove it again if you need me to." He reached for his waistband and began to unbuckle his belt right there in the middle of Hot Rides.

"Are you crazy?" She lunged for him and slapped her hand over his, which only meant she was a fraction of an inch from touching his dick, which was waking up faster at the prospect.

"Probably." He stared at the ceiling, blew out a breath, then fixed himself before spinning away.

"It's not that I don't find you attractive." Devra sighed. "But I'm—"

"Married. I know." Quinn got pissed. At himself. He knew better than to do shit like that. Coming on to her when Trevon wasn't around was a cardinal sin. He didn't plan to cheat on anybody. He just was getting so comfortable around them, he'd started to think of them as his and him as theirs instead of a handy third for threesomes. "I'm sorry. I'm used to being around my brother and the rest of his asshole friends. I wasn't thinking. You're not one of the guys, you're Trevon's wife. I promise that won't happen again."

He looked in her direction, hoping it was forgiveness instead of shock, anger, or—worse—revulsion he saw. Instead, her face drained of color as she stared, guilty as fuck, at the opening to the garage.

Trevon was standing there, silhouetted by the late afternoon sun behind him.

"Whatever you heard, that was my fault." Quinn slapped his hand to his chest. "I was being inappropriate."

"Well, don't let me stop you." Trevon shrugged. "What Devra does and with whom she does it is up to her. I'm her husband, not her owner."

"You wouldn't care if I slept with her? Even if you weren't around?" Quinn had a hard time believing that.

"I'd much rather watch." Trevon adjusted his junk. "But that's her call."

"You'd want to see that? Me and Quinn?" Devra sounded surprised and interested by the idea. "I figured it was different. You know, you and I can do the same things he and I could. When you're with him, he can give you things I can't."

"Same goes for you and him. He's a different man than I am," Trevon said softly. "He's sexy, and wild, and...in charge."

"You forgot greedy as fuck. Because if we keep talking about this, it's going to be a thing. I'm about to fuck the shit out of your wife right here, right now." Quinn was starting to think this day was about to go from boring to spectacular in less time than it took for him to get fully hard.

"I don't blame you." Trevon smiled. "She *is* incredible. And if that's what she wants, that's what you should do."

Devra looked to Quinn and nibbled her lip. "Are you sure?"

"Of course." Trevon nodded. "He's pretty good at it, you know. I can tell you from experience."

Enough talking. Quinn shifted gears, preparing to take them to the next level. It might have been reckless, but he couldn't turn down a chance to have something he'd been dreaming about for weeks.

Devra. Her burgundy lips and the deep flush around her nipples. The dark hair on her mound. And the sounds she'd made that day when he'd fucked Trevon while Trevon pleased her. They'd haunted him.

He wanted a chance to inspire those noises himself. "Trevon, close up. We've got some private business to attend to."

The guy did as he was told quickly and efficiently. He flipped the sign from *Open* to *Closed*, then smacked the button that controlled the garage doors. They rolled down, darkening the inside of the building and shutting with a clang.

"What if Gavyn comes back?" Devra whispered.

"Then he'll know what I've felt like over and over. After all the times I've walked in on Tom and Ms. Brown or who knows what combination of the Hot Rods getting it on, they fucking owe me one." He gripped Devra's ass and squeezed it, drawing her tight to his body so she could feel his hard-on between her legs. "I need this. I need you. Now. Get over here."

She dropped her magazine and joined him in his bay.

Work would never be the same after this. He'd always remember this moment and how she was staring up at him with blatant anticipation.

"Take her clothes off," Quinn said to Trevon, who came closer and eagerly did as he was told.

Devra stood there naked and unashamed. She stood tall. Well, tall for someone of her stature. He loved how proud she seemed, and how defiant.

That part wasn't going to last. She'd melt all over him soon enough.

Quinn dropped his jeans and ripped off his own shirt. That was plenty to free his cock and get the job done. Today wasn't about finesse. It was about urgency and the intensity of his desire. He reached for Devra and dragged her to him, putting his hands on her ass and lifting her.

Her hands flew to his shoulders to balance herself, but she didn't really settle in until she wrapped her legs around his waist. They were getting closer.

The hard tips of her breasts poked his chest, making it clear she'd been as horny as he had.

Why hadn't she said anything before? He'd have been happy to service her or watch Trevon do it instead. Just in case, he asked Trevon, "Is she wet?"

The other man came up behind Devra, kissing the back of her neck as he slid a hand beneath her and probed her pussy for Quinn.

"Soaked." Trevon groaned. "Can I taste her?"

"Only a little. Then I have to be inside her." Quinn thought that was generous considering how amped he was and the fact that Trevon could have her any time he and Devra liked. "Hurry."

Trevon knelt on the hard concrete. He must have done something then because Devra moaned and squirmed enough that Quinn was glad she was petite and that he had a good grip on her lithe body. A few more seconds and he barked, "Enough. Trevon, put my cock in her. Now."

The other man's huge hand surrounded Quinn. It was warm and a little rough on his erection. Perfect. Trevon tipped Quinn's dick up and aimed it at Devra, rubbing it against her core before nestling the head in the slick folds of her pussy.

"Damn, you weren't kidding." Quinn groaned. "She's so slippery. And hot."

"For you," Trevon murmured.

"For you both," Devra corrected. "Now someone better fuck me before I go crazy. Please."

She didn't have to ask Quinn twice. He'd seen how Trevon's self-control had inadvertently made her doubt her appeal. She'd never have to wonder if he wanted her or how much. He was about to show her and he'd do it as often as it took for her to believe it.

Quinn held her waist and thrust upward. It took a few tries to work himself inside her deep enough to really fuck her without being in danger of falling out. A couple of times he did and Trevon was there to put him back in Devra's pussy.

While they ground together, he tipped his head down and kissed her.

She surprised him when she bit his lower lip, goading him to ramp up his efforts.

He rocked his hips, clenching his ass to thrust into her even as he let gravity drag her down. Over and over, he stroked into her as they made out, and Trevon ran his hands over their sides and the places where they connected.

It was amazing. But it wasn't enough. Not yet.

Quinn tried to separate himself from Devra, but she clung to him and whimpered.

"I'm not going far. I just need to get...deeper." Quinn grunted on one final thrust before withdrawing from heaven. "Trevon, keep her steady. Turn her around."

He did as told, giving Quinn time to regroup.

"Devra, put your palms on the toolbox. Bend over. Stick out your ass and hold on." She followed orders pretty damn well herself. Quinn wondered, for a fleeting moment, if this was one reason they'd had so much trouble coming together. They both enjoyed a dominant touch. It could be problematic for a couple, he'd imagine.

Then he didn't care anymore. Because Devra's pussy was there, waiting for him to return.

He held his cock at the base and tapped it against her clit a few times before rubbing the blunt head up and down her slit. Then he looked at Trevon and asked, "Should I fuck her some more?"

"Yes. Harder," Trevon answered. He was beside his wife, supporting her, holding her up and telling her over and over how gorgeous she was and how much she obviously pleased Quinn.

Who was Quinn to argue?

He plunged into Devra's waiting channel, which rippled along his length at his re-entry.

She hugged him deep within her, though he didn't let that stop him from drilling in and out of her despite the undulating ring of muscles at her core. Their skin slapped together and even her perky breasts bounced as he rode her furiously.

The sound inspired him to spank her, playfully at first

then harder when she groaned his name and began to pulse around him. She was coming already. Shit.

Quinn pulled out before she could end their fun too soon.

He growled at Trevon, "Watch her. Don't let her fall."

Quinn knew he should be gentler. More patient. But it was impossible. He'd waited so long for this moment, and she brought out something primal in him that he was a little hesitant to unleash. If Trevon hadn't been there, he never would have let go like this.

No matter what, he knew the other guy would protect his wife and make sure Quinn didn't get too out of control. At least any rougher than she seemed to like it.

As if to prove his unspoken point, Devra moaned and began rubbing her clit. "More. Can I have more?"

Quinn blinked as he studied the woman Devra had transformed into and the man she was married to, who seemed to like the new her every bit as much as Quinn did.

"Come on, Quinn. Fuck my wife. Give it to her hard and fast like she likes it. Dirty. Raw. Rough." Trevon groaned. "I love watching you do this to her and drive her wild, especially since...that's not how I am. I could never give her what you're giving her."

"My cock? Yours is a hell of a lot bigger than mine." Quinn couldn't think very clearly, but what Trevon was saying seemed important. He filed it away to think about later. When he wasn't about to be buried in the tightest, hottest pussy he'd ever had the privilege to fuck again.

"It's how you use it," Trevon said with a grin.

As if to prove his point, Devra moaned as aftershocks ran through her.

Quinn was about to ramp things up even more. He

handed her over to Trevon while he got adjusted. He boosted himself up so he was sitting on top of the industrial-grade toolbox. He barked to Trevon, "Pull out that drawer."

When the guy did so, Quinn planted his booted feet in it, then curled a finger toward his palm twice in the classic gesture for *give it to me*. In this case, it was she. Devra.

Trevon lifted her effortlessly, as if she was even more petite than she really was, and positioned her so that she was sitting in Quinn's lap, facing away from him. His cock impaled her as her ass came to rest on his thighs.

"Fuck. You're so hot," he rasped against her neck, just below her ear, scraping his teeth over the sensitive skin there. Quinn grabbed her under her thighs, just above her knees, and spread her wide.

Devra cried out and arched her back, trying to work herself over Quinn's cock. She threw one hand out behind her to support some of her weight. Between that and him holding her, she was able to make some progress, working her pussy over his shaft, but not enough.

Quinn wasn't going to be able to do this forever, but he figured it wasn't going to take long to set them both off. This was the sexiest, most scandalous thing he had ever experienced.

Fortunately, Trevon seemed eager to help them along. He took up his post between their legs and bent down to lick Devra's pussy while Quinn fucked up into it, hard and fast. They worked in unison, Trevon's fluttering tongue sometimes glancing off the base of Quinn's cock or even his balls.

Devra went wild. She shrieked and ground herself on him even as Trevon reached up to make sure she didn't fall. He used the contact to fondle her breast, alternating palpating it and pinching her nipple before switching to the other one.

They were racing toward the finish line and neither of them seemed likely to lose.

Free and feral, Quinn uncovered a whole new side of Devra that he instantly fell in love with. To see her like this, so uninhibited, strong, and assertive, made him proud of her and how far she'd come since arriving at Hot Rides.

That thought alone had Quinn's balls tightening. They crept up toward his core as he gritted his teeth to keep from coming before Devra had taken her fill.

"Trevon," he groaned. "Eat her. Make her come all over your face. You know you want her to."

"Mmm," the other man agreed.

Sweat gathered on Quinn's brow. He pumped into her again and again, each time plunging to the limits of her welcoming body. But it wasn't until he grabbed a fistful of her hair and used it to pull her head back that she quaked around him.

"You like that?" he asked.

She tried to nod, but only groaned when the motion tugged harder at her scalp.

"Good. Me, too." He smiled from an inch away before capturing her mouth in a coarse kiss that was nothing like the one they'd shared while he was fucking her husband.

It was savage and sweet, because it meant that he knew she could handle it.

As if that was the most arousing thing he could have done to her, she shattered.

Devra screamed into his mouth and rode him like he was a bucking bronco. Quinn couldn't resist the rhythmic clenching of her pussy, which clamped around him even as he continued to pound into her. He shuddered, too. His balls clamped then released, launching streams of his come deep into her. Later they'd have to talk about the fact that he hadn't worn a condom—with either of them, a first for him. Right then, he didn't give a shit. It felt too good to claim her as he had her husband earlier.

His orgasm seemed like it went on forever, milked dry by her pussy spasming around him and Trevon's hand, which massaged his balls through the entire thing. The man was jerking himself off as fast and furiously as Quinn and Devra had been fucking.

"You want some help with that?" Quinn asked, out of breath.

"No." Trevon grunted. "Don't need help. Just need…"

"What?" Devra asked, in a sultry, dazed voice.

"Lift her. Off you." Trevon panted to Quinn.

Although he wasn't quite ready to leave her silky heat, Quinn did. His cock slipped free and bobbed between them. Trevon was there in a flash, cleaning every dot of Devra's arousal and his own come off the shaft and head with long, lush laps of his tongue.

"Oh fuck." Quinn would have let his head drop back, but then he wouldn't be able to watch the other man devour the evidence of Quinn's passion from his wife, because surely…yes, that's where he was going next.

Trevon put one long finger in Devra's pussy, making her moan and spasm again. He swirled it around inside her before drawing it out, crooked. Quinn's hot come dribbled out around it and Trevon was there to clean it up. He ingested every drop of their mingled fluids, groaning while he swallowed it down.

His hand flew over his fat cock. And when he'd consumed as much as he could find, the muscles in

Trevon's back rippled. His ass clenched and his cock, which had never looked bigger than right then, jutted from his fist.

Devra noticed, too. "Yes, Trevon. Come for us. Show us how much you liked it when Quinn filled me up. You liked it when he fucked your wife's pretty pussy, didn't you?"

Holy shit.

If Quinn hadn't come so recently, he'd have lost it.

Just like Trevon did.

The tall man stood straight and roared. He unleashed his pent up desire, stroking his cock even as it erupted, messing up Devra and Quinn where he'd so painstakingly cleaned them, moments before. He came so hard and so long that Quinn was a little jealous of the epic orgasm.

"Damn, Trevon," he muttered his appreciation, then gathered Devra against his chest. She curled up there in his lap like a contented kitten, though she never took her eyes off her husband.

"Sorry." Trevon gasped before bracing himself on the toolbox. "Sorry. It's just...you're so gorgeous. Both of you. That was amazing."

"It was." Quinn agreed. But now he felt the darkness encroaching.

He shifted, feeling the urge to move lest he get too comfortable there, with them.

Quinn held Devra out and Trevon was there to take her, lowering her to the ground while keeping her steady in the circle of his strong arms. They put their foreheads together and stared into each other's eyes with goofy grins on their faces.

That was Quinn's signal. It was time for him to leave them alone so they could bond and grow tighter, without him.

Trevon was tending to Devra, and she was doing the same for him, bringing each other slowly back to reality as they descended from their euphoric high. Quinn sighed as he watched them together and wished it could be him doing that for them. And have them do the same for him. Reassure him that this was more than a simple physical transaction where they exchanged orgasms but nothing higher than the waist or deeper than the surface of their skin.

No hearts, no minds, and definitely no emotions. None of that stuff.

He edged toward the door, feeling like shit even after one of the best climaxes of his life. It was getting harder and harder to go each time he had to peel himself away from them and the pure bliss they were able to create together.

Quinn had one hand on the doorknob when he heard Devra ask Trevon, "Where is he? Not again. Trevon, don't let him leave us."

Trevon's head snapped up and his lion's eyes stared straight at Quinn as if daring him to walk out on him and his wife. He said simply, "Stay."

"I can't." Quinn shook his head, but neither could he make his fucking wrist turn that knob.

"What if we need you?" Trevon asked.

Quinn practically snarled, feeling cornered. "What if I need to go? For my own sanity?"

"Then you're going to need to explain why." Devra walked toward him on wobbly legs. "Because this hurts me. It hurts us."

"I didn't figure you for a coward," Trevon said.

Quinn huffed out a sigh. "Then you figured wrong."

"You've helped us overcome our fears about what

we're capable of giving each other. You should let us do the same for you." Devra reached out and removed his hand from the door, prying it up finger by finger.

"Whatever you're running from can't be as bad as what we've been through." Trevon meant well, but he had no idea what Quinn had endured. Of course their situation had been worse, but his hadn't been a walk in the park either. Maybe that was part of what made him feel ashamed about the pain he still harbored when they'd withstood so much more without crumbling. "We can do more for you than get you off, you know?"

"Talk to us," Devra demanded.

"Then if you still want to walk away, walk away." Trevon shrugged, as if it was no big deal. "At least then we'll understand why."

23

Quinn couldn't stay. But they wouldn't let him leave either. How was he going to keep himself from falling in love with them if he couldn't put some distance—physical and emotional—between them and what they'd just shared? It got more intense every single time.

Things were getting serious no matter how hard he tried to keep them about sex and facilitating the blossoming relationship between Devra and Trevon.

He looked at the garage door, calculating his odds of sprinting past Trevon before the other guy tackled him. They weren't very good. Trevon was so tall and lanky, he had a hell of a reach. Besides, Quinn was wiped out from how hard he'd come.

Again.

They'd shared the best orgasms of his life with him. And more.

"If you only want something physical, I guess that's fine. You don't owe us anything other than a good time,"

Trevon said. "Just don't treat us—especially Devra—like sex toys and leave us once you've gotten your fill."

"No. It's not okay." Devra contradicted her husband. She had grown some balls lately, and Quinn loved it. It was one of the things that made him feel like he hadn't totally fucked up by sleeping with them. "It's disrespectful of our feelings. We care about you, Quinn. When you take off like what we've done was only about the orgasms, it's rude and kind of...demeaning. Something I might have expected of men I used to know. Not you."

"That was never my intention." Quinn swallowed hard. It was time to come clean. He'd seen the devastation Roman had unintentionally wrought on Carver, his husband, when they were working through the kinks in their relationship, and Quinn never wanted to do the same to someone he cared for. So he manned up and exposed his emotions. He only wished it was as easy to do that as it was to flaunt his naked body.

"It's difficult for me to feel all the things I do toward you and know that I'm not really a part of your relationship. I would never want to entangle myself so much that I risk pulling you two apart instead of pushing you together when things end."

"Who says this has to stop?" Devra asked quietly. "It hasn't for Sally and her guys or the rest of the Hot Rods and their group activities. Why do you think it will with you?"

"Because..." Fuck it. He might as well say it. "No one's ever loved me like that. Not enough to keep me."

He spun around and braced himself on the workbench, his stomach aching like someone had pummeled him with an invisible fist from his past.

"Quinn." Devra put her hand on his back and stroked

him gently. "It might seem that way, but I'm sure that's not true. What about your brother and the Hot Rods?"

"They took care of me when I was a kid. I love them to the bottom of my soul, but they have their own lives and their own relationships. I always felt like an outsider to that. Even with Tom and Ms. Brown, when they got married. I sometimes stayed in my room at their house and the rest of the time in the Hot Rods' living room because I didn't want to be a burden on anyone for too long in case they decided I was inconvenient and kicked me out. I knew they needed their space. I don't hold that against them."

Quinn shook his head. "That's just how it is. I've never really belonged anywhere. Hell, even here Gavyn and Amber helped me build my own separate space, away from their own house. I'm grateful, I am. I just..."

"You were on your own when all of them had a partner." Trevon rested his hip against the workbench and put his hand on Quinn's shoulder. Their soothing touches did make him feel better, even though he knew he shouldn't count on them being there to prop him up forever.

"Yeah." He nodded. Figured he'd fall in love with two people who already were attached. Even if it was to each other.

"Can I ask you something personal?" Devra wondered.

Quinn laughed at that. "I'm pretty sure you can considering I was buried inside you five minutes ago."

"I get the feeling this discussion is a lot more intimate to you than sex," she murmured.

Of course she would understand.

He rubbed his temples. "Can we go outside at least? I need to breathe if we're going to talk about this shit."

When he spun around, Trevon took one of his hands and Devra the other. They led him from Hot Rides and out onto the grass beyond the blacktopped lot. A little farther down, there was a stream and a bench Gavyn had put there. He called it his thinking spot.

Quinn knew it was really where he went to find his zen when he was trying to resist the compulsion for a drink. It seemed appropriate to sit there now, sandwiched between the two biggest temptations Quinn had ever had in his life.

He drew a giant breath, released it, and then said, "What do you want to know, Devra?"

She leaned her head on his upper arm. "You talk about 'coming' to Hot Rods as a teenager. Where were you before that?"

"Locked in the attic of my mom's house, probably." Quinn said it because it was true, not because he was trying to shock his lovers. However, it seemed to have that effect.

It was sad that he didn't quite realize how fucked up his past was compared to people with normal lives and normal families.

"Don't worry, it's not as bad as it sounds." Quinn couldn't say why he was covering for the woman, even now. Probably because she was the only mother he'd ever have, even if she was a shitty one. "When I was up there, I was safe from her drunken rages and those of her boyfriends—though that's a piss poor term for people you sleep with for booze money."

"Oh, Quinn." Devra snuggled closer to his side, as if she could infuse him with some of her warmth. He could feel how cold and clammy his hands had gotten from talking about this stuff again.

"No wonder you were so kind to us," Trevon said. "You know, a lot of people were aware of our situation and probably felt bad, but no one helped us like you did. No one offered us a way to make ourselves whole and independent again. You've never once judged us or our situations."

Quinn nodded, swallowing hard. "I didn't really think of it like that, but yeah, I know what it's like to be poor and fighting to make it through another day. How you start to lose hope that things could ever change."

He didn't say it out loud, but people could only take so much. There came a point where any rational person would consider if it was better to end things than to keep going on like you were when you were suffering daily.

"It can take a long time to get past something like that. To build a new life and learn to stand on your own. Even with people who support you and give you as much patience, understanding, and opportunity as they can afford. I thought I was there." Quinn cleared his throat.

Opening up to Devra and Trevon in the bedroom, and now rehashing his past...well, that was bringing back a lot of emotions he thought he'd buried. He was terrified of being left alone again.

"How did you finally escape so you could start over?" Devra asked.

"My brother Roman had it worse when he was a kid. A bunch of broken bones from beatings, but our mother got smarter after he ran away. Like I said, she kept me locked in when she wasn't around so I couldn't leave, even if she hadn't brainwashed me into believing I had to stay. There are fancy terms for this bullshit that I learned in the counseling Tom and Roman made me go to, but let's be honest. I was a kid. She was my mom. The one person who's supposed to take care of you. She mostly hurt me in ways that couldn't be so easily called out and held against her. Ways that didn't require institutionalized medical attention, which gets documented for minors."

It was one of the reasons the abuse had continued so long. They had neighbors who hadn't even known he existed. Hell, Roman hadn't even had a clue of Quinn's existence. He'd been like a sad, lonely ghost haunting the attic of that house.

Trevon punched his thigh, making Quinn wince. "It's okay. It was a long time ago and the kid I was has been gone for years. Because Roman found me. He saw me in the window one day and refused to leave me behind. He busted down the door of our mother's house. She came home when he was trying to convince me that we were family and that I'd be safe with him. I didn't believe him at first. Couldn't wrap my brain around the possibility it was true. Fuck, I almost got him killed for his efforts. There were shots fired and he had to run. I thought I'd lost any chance I had, but he—and Tom and the rest of the Hot Rods..."

Quinn's throat started to tighten. His eyes closed and his nose burned with pent up grief.

"They rescued you." Devra couldn't get close enough by his side, so she straddled him, sat on his lap facing him and wrapped her arms around him. Trevon hugged him, too. They surrounded him with strength he didn't have right then, lending him some of their own.

"Roman came back for me." Quinn couldn't stop the single tear from escaping the corner of his eye. "He came back."

Devra was stroking his hair, whispering reminders to

him that he was safe and everything was okay. But was it really?

He shook his head, opening his eyes and taking in concerned gazes from both Trevon and Devra. "If we keep doing this, I'm going to fall for you both. If what we're doing helps fix what's broken between you and you don't need me anymore, that's okay. I understand. I came into this knowing you two were already a unit. I want what's best for you, no matter what. But I've got to look out for myself, too. There's no one else to do it for me."

"You're scared," Devra murmured.

Quinn nodded and groaned. He might as well put it all out there at this point. "What if I lose you? What if I end up alone again?"

"You won't," Trevon promised. He was still clutching Quinn's hand like he didn't plan to let go anytime soon. Or maybe ever. "We want to look out for you, too."

"Like you've done for us," Devra agreed. "No relationship is guaranteed. But even if we stop sleeping together, I swear we'll be there for you. You're a part of our lives now, part of our family, for good."

Quinn felt selfish and a little embarrassed for getting so upset. It wasn't like he had no one. He had Roman, Gavyn, and the rest of his Hot Rods and Hot Rides family. But he wanted to be more than the runt of the litter. He wanted to start his own clan, starting with a partner or partners who were strong enough to stand by his side for life.

Mostly he was petrified that he'd found exactly that and he didn't want to blow it.

"If we're going to keep doing this, it has to be about more than simple sex." Devra looked at Quinn and

Trevon. "I care about you both. It's already too late for me. You hear what I'm saying?"

Both of the guys nodded. Devra was braver than both of them to admit it so easily.

Quinn stood up, then set Devra on her feet even as Trevon got to his beside them. He grabbed them each by the hand and pulled them back up the hill.

"Where are you taking us?" Devra asked with a sly smile that was outrageous given how well he'd fucked her earlier.

"We're going home." He marched straight for his house and hoped they realized that he meant they'd be staying together at his place. Now, *their* place. For the foreseeable future.

Sharing their lives, not only his bed.

He prayed this wasn't the dumbest decision he'd made yet. It would wound him a hell of a lot more than some broken bones if he lost Trevon and Devra now.

24

Devra kicked back in the swivel chair that had become her outpost in the Hot Rides office over the past several weeks. It had been almost a month since the day she and Quinn had sex in the garage and everything had changed between the three of them.

It was the first time in years, maybe ever, she could remember feeling so...peaceful and relaxed. Comfortable in her own skin and where she was in life. She had a best friend who was her husband and another who was her lover. Plus, she'd spent a lot of time with the Hot Rods ladies, who supported her as she figured out how to navigate the complex relationship they'd landed themselves in.

They were back on track with their savings and financial goals. Someday not too long from now, they'd be able to afford the legal and filing fees for her green card. They even had a consultation scheduled for two weeks from now with a lawyer Tom had recommended.

Trevon had asked her last night if she still had dreams

of finishing school and opening her restaurant. Those had been impossible not too long ago. She'd let them wither and die because it was less painful than constantly being upset that they were out of reach.

And now...both Quinn and Trevon had revived those aspirations and helped her believe that anything was possible. She figured it was true what people said... If you gave up when everything was miserable, you'd stay at your lowest point and never find your way to a better place.

She smiled as she watched Quinn and Trevon collaborating on some of the few remaining details of the Indian restoration. Sally had dropped off the fuel tank, fenders, and some other stuff Devra didn't know the names for, freshly painted. The woman was as talented as she was a good friend. The bike looked clean, fresh, and definitely less than eighty years old while maintaining its original design and style.

Trevon was going to look so good riding it. He'd be grinning as he remembered the badass his pop had once been and followed in his footsteps or tire tracks. Especially if he had Quinn riding next to him. They made her mouth dry and other parts of her wet without even trying. Not only because they were sexy, but because they were competent, kind, and untamed.

She was willing to admit to herself after living together with them these past weeks that she loved them.

Both of them. And she was pretty sure the feeling was mutual by the way they looked at her and touched her. This had been the hottest summer of her life and it had barely gotten started.

Damn. She shifted in her chair.

Devra had to distract herself, so she picked up the appointment book Gavyn and Quinn had relied on for so long and started inputting some of their chicken scratch into the simple program Amber had installed on the shop computer. The woman was a business guru, so it must have killed her that her husband refused to implement a lot of her suggestions, until now.

Amber had thanked her and full-on kissed her on the cheek when Devra had offered to help the guys get their shit together. It wasn't like she had anything better to do, while Amber was busy running her own company. Besides, it gave her ideas about how to organize her restaurant...someday.

"What're you up to in here?" Quinn asked as he dropped off his notes on the service he'd performed. She'd type it up for him so the customer could actually read what it was he was charging them for.

"You know, just tidying up after you guys." She shook her head. "The usual."

"Hey, I'll have you know I'm very neat." Quinn crossed his arms with mock offense.

It was true—he kept his house spotless, and his tools were organized as well as a surgeon's instruments. She pointed to the garage bay through the large glass window separating the spaces. "Maybe out there. Not in here."

"This is bullshit paperwork." He waved it off.

She laughed. "Then I guess it's a good thing you have me."

"Do I have you?" he asked. Slivers of his insecurity showed through every once in a while. She and Trevon were doing their best to prove to him that they weren't going to abandon him. He was part of them now, at least as far as she was concerned.

"You do." She stood then and put her arms up around his neck.

His hands flew to her waist, keeping her steady and close.

Behind him, Trevon had glanced over as if he had some kind of sexdar. He grinned and flashed her a thumbs-up. So Devra went onto her tiptoes and kissed Quinn sweetly.

No hurry. No desperation.

Only gentle, reassuring affection. She and Trevon had conspired to show him over and over that they cared. Maybe soon he would realize what he was coming to mean to them.

Lost in the sweet kiss, she didn't hear any approaching vehicles. The jingle of the bell on the door startled her. She broke apart from Quinn with a lurch that left him holding nothing in his hands. He blinked, his eyes filling with sorrow.

She'd have to fix that later. After she dealt with the customer.

A man stood on the welcome mat, thick arms crossed, legs spread apart as he shot them a disapproving frown from his craggy better-days face. The disgust in his stare was apparent.

Devra decided to ignore it and added extra politeness to her voice when she said, "Hello. How can I help you?"

"Where's Gavyn?" he barked.

Okay, rude. But whatever. "I'm sorry, sir. He's not available right now. May I take a message?"

His beady black eyes narrowed. "What kind of accent is that?"

Devra paused. "Excuse me?"

"I know a sand monkey when I see one. I come to this shop because the guys who own it are red-blooded Americans and I can be sure I'm giving my hard-earned cash to good people. Guess not anymore. Fucking traitors."

Shock caused her knees to bend and she plopped back into the office chair at the front desk. Sure, some ignorant people had shunned her and mistreated her in more subtle and hurtful ways since she'd been in this country. But rarely before had she faced such blatant and barefaced hate on sight or sound simply for where she came from.

"You won't be coming to Hot Rides for jack shit anymore." Quinn stepped in front of Devra. He planted his boots in a wide-set stance. The silver skull ring on his finger glinted in the sunlight when he balled his hands into fists. His tattoos seemed to come alive as the muscles beneath them bunched and flexed. "You're not welcome here. I suggest you leave before I do something we're both going to regret."

About that time, Trevon opened the shop door. "Is everything okay?"

"No," Quinn and Devra said in unison.

"This fuckface was about to leave." Quinn pointed toward the door, but the guy couldn't resist one final parting shot.

"It's illegals like you taking all the jobs in Middletown." The man shook his head, revulsion twisting his features into something so ugly Devra could hardly stand to look at him. "What a shame. I thought this place was better than that."

"What the fuck did you just say to my wife?" Trevon snarled as he advanced, stopped only by Quinn putting a hand on his chest and keeping him at bay.

The man looked at Trevon's ring finger, then to Devra.

"Figures she's yours. Do you know your boss man is taking his fill of her, too?"

And that was all Quinn could stomach, apparently.

"Get the fuck out of here, you racist, closed-minded asshole." Quinn grabbed the man by the collar of his plaid shirt and hauled him to the front door, which he kicked open before flinging the man out into the parking lot.

The man tripped over his brown construction boots and landed on his ass. He scrambled to his feet, but slunk away instead of coming back for more.

"It says a lot when you'd rather have people like them than people like me in your establishment. I'll be leaving a review that says so on all the internet sites, too. You'll be lucky if I don't sue you for putting your hands on me." The guy dusted himself off as he rose. He spit on the ground before climbing into his pickup truck and squealing out of the driveway.

Devra deflated. Pure adrenaline and indignation melted into fear, agony, and embarrassment.

"Fuck. I'm sorry." Quinn turned and rushed to Devra.

Trevon was there, too. He lifted her from the chair and wrapped her in his arms. Of course he understood. He'd faced people's groundless revulsion himself plenty. It was one of the things that had attracted them to each other. They understood what it was like to be...other.

She hadn't realized she was trembling until she was sandwiched between the solid bodies of Quinn and Trevon. They held her and rocked her until her shock turned into grief. No matter how hard she worked or what the circumstances were, there were people in the world who would mistreat her simply because of where she'd been born, or Trevon because of the color of his skin.

Fuck that. They weren't worth less than anyone else.

Even though she knew that, it was still hard not to sometimes listen to those lies. Today was one thing, blatant and easier to dismiss despite the shock and pain the encounter had caused. Other times it was more subtle and ultimately more painful.

These beliefs were so ingrained in people's subconscious that they didn't always even realize they were adhering to them. Instead, they ignored the suffering of their fellow human beings, blaming the victim for their unfortunate situation instead of circumstances. Having lived on both sides of the fence, Devra knew what a difference head starts and privileges she'd taken for granted before made.

Quinn hadn't had exactly the same experiences, but he'd never turned a blind eye to their suffering. He'd offered her and Trevon a hand up so they could be productive. He'd invited them into his life as surely as Trevon and his family had welcomed Devra alone.

One day, maybe their love and compassion—and that of others like them—would outshine the shadows in the world. But until then, she was glad to have the sanctuary of these two men's open arms to take shelter in.

"Fuck this." Quinn seemed as overwhelmed as she felt. "We're taking the rest of the day off. Let's go home so I can remind you both what I love about you."

Devra's heart skipped a beat and Trevon's arms twitched against her. She looked up at him and flashed him a watery smile. It was happening. They were becoming one unit like they'd hoped they would.

Together, the three of them could face the world, including the ugly parts.

25

Devra breathed deep, enjoying the scent of the woods surrounding Hot Rides and the wildflowers that were in full bloom in the tall grass at the edge of the trees. It was beautiful, tranquil, and definitely her happy place.

Hot Rides had become her happy place.

Anywhere Trevon and Quinn were would be fine, but this...this was paradise.

She took her time strolling down the long, winding driveway to the mailbox. It was another one of those daily rituals she'd taken on to make herself feel useful. As she passed by Gavyn and Amber's house, she noticed the other woman standing out on the porch, so she waved.

"I've got some tea brewing," Amber called. "Fresh doughnuts, too. Stop by on your way back if you want."

"Of course I want!" Devra laughed and picked up the pace a bit.

She made it to the cluster of three black boxes with flames painted down the side—courtesy of Sally, she was sure—and opened the door for Hot Rides. She scooped out bills, catalogs, and coupons before moving on to Gavyn and Amber's. Might as well since she was already there and planning to hang out and chat with Amber for a while.

Next she opened Quinn's. They only had one address for the two cottages, but it didn't matter because she and Trevon never got any mail anyway. The cottages had solar power and were hooked into water and sewer through the garage, so they paid their share of the utilities directly to Gavyn. They hadn't lived there long enough to get their own junk mail either.

So it surprised her when a crisp business envelope in Quinn's box had her name on it.

What the hell?

She glanced at the return address and saw an official-looking seal along with the words *US Immigration and Customs Enforcement.* Suddenly, her appetite for strawberry-filled doughnuts vanished.

The letter flapped in her shaking hands, making it harder to rip open the back of the envelope. But when she did and pulled it out, she began to read.

All the other mail she'd been clutching in the crook of her left arm fluttered to the ground and scattered. She went numb from head to toe. For a second, she considered running. Where would she go?

She had nowhere, nothing, and nobody else but Hot Rides, Quinn, and Trevon.

So her feet began to move, then move faster. Before she knew it, she was sprinting with the poor letter crumpled in her pumping fist.

"Devra!" Amber shouted as she raced past, but she didn't stop to explain. Couldn't really since she didn't understand what it meant.

So she kept going to the only safe harbor she knew.

The familiar whir of power tools drifted toward her as she approached the shop. Even that comforting noise couldn't calm her racing heart right then.

"Trevon!" she shouted as she neared. "Quinn!"

The guys came running out to meet her, their long legs making quicker work of closing the gap between them than hers. From the door of the office, even Gavyn poked his head out to see what the ruckus was all about. They'd been on edge since that hostile customer had verbally assaulted her.

Trevon and Quinn intercepted her on the lawn, frowns and concern clouding their handsome faces. She couldn't even breathe enough to explain the problem.

"What's going on?" Trevon asked.

"Letter. From Immigration." Devra thrust it out so he could read it and explain to Quinn, too.

"They've scheduled a mandatory interview with her." Trevon scanned it again as if reading it a second time would change the ominous tone and sick feeling those words planted in her gut and probably his as well.

"But...you didn't resubmit her green card application yet, did you?" Quinn double-checked, although they'd talked about their intended timeline the night before.

Trevon shook his head. "We almost have enough. A few more weeks, probably, before I'll have the fee. I'm sorry."

She hugged him in an attempt to smother his remorse, then said, "I know. We're working on it. But...then, why? Why do they want to talk to me? Why not us together? Have we waited too long to apply? Did I break some rule we don't know about?"

"Fuck! I don't think so, but I'm not sure. The laws are

complicated as fuck. As far as I know, there's not a time limitation. But I've been wrong before." Trevon started pacing, his brow furrowed as he read the letter again and again, just like she had.

No matter how much he stared at it, he wouldn't find the answer to their questions. She hadn't.

"It's probably nothing, guys." Quinn stepped between them and grabbed each of them by the wrist. He pulled them together and put his arms around them both. "I hate to see you freaking out like this over a stupid letter."

"If something's wrong...these days..." Trevon cursed. "They could send her home. Deport her. And we wouldn't be able to do shit about it. People, like that fuckwad that came in here a few weeks ago, they're stirring up misplaced aggression, and innocent survivors like Devra are paying the price. This is bad. Really bad."

"Devra's not going anywhere," Quinn promised Trevon, his voice steely. Then he looked down at her. "You're not going anywhere. Neither of you are."

"I have a bad feeling about this, too," Devra said around the lump in her throat that was threatening to cut off her breath. "Something's not right."

"Okay. Here's what we'll do: I'm going to call Alanso. He's dealt with this stuff before. He's from Cuba and his mom had...issues with the process. He knows a lot about this shit. Maybe he even knows of a lawyer we can hire." Quinn was too busy finding a solution to notice Devra and Trevon's faces falling.

"We can't afford—" Devra began before Quinn cut her off with a kiss. It was desperate and hard, but it kept her from saying it.

"*We* can." He gestured between the three of them. "You are my people now, like you keep saying that I'm yours. I will fight for you as hard as anyone else I consider my family. Like Roman fought for me. I'm going to call."

Devra wanted to believe him. Except she knew that no matter how hard he battled, he couldn't possibly win against the government or popular opinion. If they kicked her out, she'd have to go.

She'd lose Trevon, Quinn, her happy place, and—quite possibly—her life.

26

Quinn flew along the twisty road that linked Hot Rides and Hot Rods. He set a new personal best time for traveling the distance between the shops. Panic clawed at him. Things had been going so well, he should have known it couldn't last.

He pulled up to the garage, skidding the last few feet, and jumped off his motorcycle practically before he'd come to a complete stop. With his stomach in knots, he strode into the shop and looked around frantically for his brother.

"Hey Quinnigans." Nola smiled and meandered closer with her arms open for a hug.

He needed one, but he was afraid to take it in case he lost his shit. So he backed away and shook his head. "Where's Roman?"

"He went for a ride with Carver. Probably getting a BJ on the side of the road somewhere. They should be back soon." She started to catch on to his agitation. "Everything okay?"

"I don't know." He tugged on his hair. "Alanso then. I need Al."

"He commandeered that empty room in the back corner for a welding lesson with Wren." Nola winced. "Enter at your own risk. They were super geeked up and wearing all kinds of protective gear. They mentioned the threat of setting yourself on fire if you bug them."

"It's kind of an emergency." At least it felt that way to him. He'd love to be wrong, though.

Nola frowned then. "Should I round everyone up?"

Quinn nodded. He needed his family. The only people who'd never left him.

"It's going to be okay. Whatever it is." Nola put her hand on his forearm and squeezed. "We're here for you."

Except it wasn't himself he was most concerned about.

He jogged to the back room and through a shower of sparks. Wren Asbery, the best and finest welder in the entire state, was huddled over a piece of aluminum, face shield firmly in place as she mentored Alanso, who was practicing. Specialty welding—stainless and aluminum— was a skill they paid her very well for from time to time.

They'd talked about bringing someone in-house to be a dedicated resource but hadn't found the right fit yet. If only Wren would take them up on their offer to come work for Hot Rods and Hot Rides, they wouldn't have to spend time learning how to do it half as well as she did.

Quinn waved his arms. Wren noticed and tapped Alanso on the shoulder. He stopped and turned to figure out what had interrupted his lesson. They both stood upright when they saw Quinn standing there like the hot mess he was at that moment.

Wren had nearly a foot on Alanso in height, though

she probably weighed less than the Hot Rods' engine expert. Where Alanso was dark, thanks to his Cuban genes, Wren was like an iconic angel. Maybe one of those kind of scary avenging angels, though. She had long, platinum blond hair and eyes that were the lightest gray possible. They seemed to spear into Quinn as soon as she flipped up her face shield. "What's wrong?"

Was it that obvious?

Alanso whipped off his mask as well. The smile that had crossed his face on seeing Quinn faded fast.

"I need a lawyer," Quinn said. "A fucking good one."

"What the hell did you do?" Alanso's question came out dripping extra thick in his accent.

"It's not for me. It's for Devra." Quinn took the letter from his pocket and handed it to Alanso. "She got this today and it's scaring the shit out of us. Do you understand what could be happening?"

Alanso read it out loud so that Wren was up to speed, too. "I think you're right, kid. You need a lawyer."

"Hang on." Wren's lips twisted in disgust. "I think I can do one better than that. I know an ICE agent who's assigned to this regional office. And he owes me about ten billion favors."

"Sexual favors?" Alanso teased.

Wren smacked him on the back of his bald head. "Hardly."

However, the way she said it...Quinn wasn't sure she was telling the truth. He didn't give a fuck if she slept with goats so long as she could help Devra. "Please call him. I'll meet him anywhere, anytime. I need to know why she's being summoned in like this and what we're up against."

Wren used her teeth to remove her fireproof gloves,

then fished in the zipped pocket of her welding apron and withdrew her cellphone. For a man she didn't sleep with, she sure had her agent friend on a pretty easy-to-access speed dial. In less than five seconds, she said, "Jordan, I need you out at Hot Rods on the southeast side of Middletown."

She was quiet as the guy responded. Then she said, "Okay. See you in twenty."

Quinn and Alanso looked at each other, then at the tall, classy-looking blonde woman.

"Those must have been like anal-level favors," Alanso said with a laugh.

Wren sighed. "I wish it was something as simple as that. Something he could take back or make right."

"Sorry." Alanso laid off her. They all had their histories around here.

To pass the time they tried to talk about shop stuff in an attempt to distract Quinn. But all that happened was that he ended up pacing the back room and telling Alanso, Wren, and anyone else who showed up about how awesome Devra and Trevon were and the cool things they'd been up to lately.

It had been a while since he'd come home and debriefed his friends.

The entire time he rambled, more and more of the Hot Rods filled the room until they were all there. Roman came running in right around the time Eli asked quietly, "When were you going to tell us you've fallen in love with Devra?"

He shrugged.

"Her husband, too?" Roman asked as he stepped closer and flung one arm around Quinn to draw him close.

He nodded.

"We'll do everything we can to protect her, if it comes to that," Sally promised. She herself had escaped a cult. And she'd gotten close to Devra over the past month or so. She knew what was at stake here.

Long before twenty minutes had passed, a slender man with close-cropped dark hair who was even taller than Wren marched up the driveway from an intentionally non-descript black, unmarked car. He flashed his badge at Holden, the first person he saw in the garage, and whipped off his mirrored sunglasses. "Agent Mikalski. I'm looking for Wren Asbery."

"I'm here, Jordan," she called to her...frenemy? Lover?

A man didn't come running that quick unless he had some pretty strong feelings.

"Are you okay?" He scanned her from head to toe. His initial concern turned to blatant appreciation as he took in her rugged clothes, which contrasted with her appearance in every possible way.

"Fine. But him...That's Quinn, and he's got problems." She pointed, then took the letter from him and crossed to Agent Mikalski. "The woman's husband works for Quinn. She got this in the mail today. What does it mean?"

The agent glanced at the form letter and digested it faster than anyone else. Maybe he'd seen similar ones before. He frowned. "Let me make a few calls."

Tom and Ms. Brown hovered protectively near Quinn while they waited for the results. He had chewed his nail nearly to the quick before Ms. Brown put her hand over his and guided it away from his mouth. Agent Mikalski came back into the room then, his face grim.

"Just say it," Quinn told him. "Quick, before I puke."

"It seems someone sent an anonymous tip to the

immigration abuse and fraud email address reporting Devra." He cleared his throat. "You want to see the picture they took of you two making out as evidence, or was it memorable enough that you don't need the reminder?"

"Motherfucker!" Quinn knew exactly who it had been. That redneck piece of shit who'd gone on a rampage, spewing his prejudice all over the Hot Rides office.

"It gets worse. In addition to that, they filed a report that said she's working without a permit at Hot Rides motorcycle shop. I assume that's where you employ Mr. Russell?"

Quinn couldn't hear anymore after that. His ears buzzed.

"Hey." Roman guided him to a folding chair and shoved his head between his knees. "Take a deep breath. Jesus, you're too big to catch if you pass out."

When the stars faded from his vision, Quinn lifted his face toward the agent. "She isn't working for Hot Rides, but she hangs out with us every day, so sometimes if the phone rings, she'll grab it, or if a customer comes in but we're busy in the garage she'll say hello or ask them what they need. It's instinct. It wasn't a job or any shit like that."

"I'm not going to sugarcoat this." Agent Mikalski stared directly at him. "It looks bad."

"She's going to get taken away. From her husband. And me. And the life she's building here. They're going to send her back to the people and place that killed her father." His mind reeled. Why hadn't he considered the danger he was putting her in? "She's going to suffer. Trevon will be crushed. The three of us will be destroyed. And it's all *my* fault. Why do I always do this to the people I care about? I'm a fucking curse."

"Quinn..." Tom tried to approach him carefully, as if

he were a rabid animal. As he should, since Quinn was volatile and on edge.

"Can I ask...?" Agent Mikalski hesitated, looking toward Wren for guidance.

"You can speak freely around them," she told him. "They're like us."

What the fuck did that mean? Quinn whipped his head toward Wren.

She pointed to Eli, Alanso, and Sally. "Those three are married. The rest are coupled up, but there's more between them all. I've spent enough time here to see it clearly. They're polyamorous and have a special bond like we—"

Wren snapped her mouth closed then and put her hands over it. Whatever it was that had been lost between her and Agent Mikalski gutted Quinn. He might be facing the same fate.

Agent Mikalski tried to reach for her. She wrenched away from his touch, so he dropped his hand. Poor bastard. "Anyway... Are you saying that you weren't cheating on Mrs. Russell's husband and that the three of you have an equal, loving partnership?"

"We're working on it." Quinn stood. He crossed his arms and spread his legs, daring the other guy to say something bad about it. "I love them. They love each other."

No one mentioned the third, missing piece of that equation.

Did they love him? He wasn't sure, but he hoped that if they didn't yet, they might eventually.

"Then the best strategy you have is to be honest." Agent Mikalski shrugged.

"Jordan, what are the odds of that working?" Wren

looked like she wanted to curse him out or maybe punch him. Quinn had never seen her angry before. "People don't understand. They judge. And terrible things like this happen because of it. Soul mates are torn apart."

"I didn't say it's a good chance. I said it's the best tactic," Agent Mikalski shot her a glance full of compassion and longing. "Look, I can't promise anything. Wren's right, this is going to be a touchy situation. I'll see who I can talk to and what shifts I can swap so I can be the agent who interviews Mrs. Russell. At the very least, I'll try to make sure the person assigned to her case is someone who supports LGBTQ rights. Polyamory isn't recognized or protected by the law, though. So it's going to be a judgment call. Down to the day and the person and whatever other damning evidence they might have against Mrs. Russell by then. Let's be honest, in the current political climate I'm not exactly a favorite among my fellow agents and bosses—some of whom were appointed by this administration. But I'll do my best to help."

"Thank you, Jordan," Wren said softly. It seemed for a moment like she might reach out to him to touch his hand or hug him. Then she thought better of it, slapped the visor on her welding helmet down, and jerked her head toward whatever she'd been working on with Alanso, beckoning him over.

"Whatever you do," Agent Mikalski told Quinn then. "The three of you have to have your shit figured out before that appointment. If there's one bit of uncertainty or inconsistency to her story, she'll be gone. No doubt. Make sure she knows how you feel about her and that it's mutual, or you'll have to abandon this plan and come up with something else, although that photo is pretty damning. I don't know that there's any other defense that has even the pathetic likelihood of working that this approach does."

Quinn nodded. It was time to bare his heart to Devra and Trevon and figure out if they thought he was worth gambling their future on. Unfortunately, they'd already done so without realizing it.

"Another thing..." The agent stepped closer to Quinn and lowered his voice. "If you can help them out so they can file for her green card and change her status immediately that would be the best insurance you have against this ever happening again."

"I will. Thank you." Quinn shook the agent's hand a little harder than he'd intended. Adrenaline and terror still coursed through him. "Money was an issue, but I'll take care of it. I'll do anything for them."

"Must be nice." Agent Mikalski looked over Quinn's shoulder at Wren with a sad smile, as if he was snapping a mental photo that he could take out later and look at in the dark of night. "Could you do something for me?"

"Of course." Quinn didn't care what request the agent made, he would see that it was done.

"Keep an eye out for Wren. Look after her like you would Mrs. Russell." Agent Mikalski winced, then put his mirrored sunglasses on. "I hope you never find out, kid, what it's like when you're not able to do that for the one you love."

"I swear I will. For that matter, I've been trying to hire her on at Hot Rides for a while now. I'll try harder," he promised.

"She's worth twice whatever you offered her." Agent

Mikalski nodded, turned on his heel, then strode to his car. He hadn't put those sunglasses on fast enough to hide the agony in his eyes from Quinn. But Quinn wouldn't have needed to see it to feel it radiating off the man in painful waves.

Please God, don't let that be me after Devra's appointment.

27

"Hey Ollie, it's Trevon. From Hot Rides." He tried to sound casual when he felt anything but. "How's it going?"

"Another day, another trash heap." Ollie laughed. "What's up?"

"The bike is ready. Did you have any bites?" Trevon said it fast, just got it out there so he couldn't chicken out. Pop would understand. He'd loved Devra even if he met her for the first time every day.

"Sort of. I thought I had one guy on the hook. Except he could only come up with forty-eight grand cash," Ollie said. "Don't worry, though, it's worth what you're asking and then some. We'll find the right person."

"I don't have that kind of time." Trevon drew a deep breath, then said, "Get him on the phone. Tell him it's a deal if he can put the money in my bank account before the end of business today."

"What the..." Ollie sounded as if he'd taken the phone away from his ear and was staring at it like Trevon was crazy.

"I don't have time to explain. Please. It's important." Trevon couldn't bear to think what his damn error and waiting this long to sell the motorcycle might have cost Devra already.

"Okay. Give me five. I'll call you back with his answer." Ollie muttered under his breath as he disconnected.

Trevon hung up the shop phone, then wandered over to the Indian. He settled on the cushy new seat and stroked the fuel tank, saying his last goodbyes. It felt like letting go of his pop all over again.

Better that than having to watch Devra be ripped away from him. And Quinn.

The instant the phone rang, he lunged for it. "Hot Rides."

"It's done. You'll have the money in an hour or so," Ollie said. "I hope whatever you needed that cash for was worth it."

"It is. Thanks, Ollie. I really owe you one." Trevon ended the call before he could get emotional.

He looked back at the bike one last time, then turned off the lights in the garage.

When he turned to leave, Quinn was standing right in front of him, his face pale and his eyes crinkled at the corners as if he was in pain. "What did you do?"

"What I had to." Trevon shrugged as if it was no big deal when his heart felt like it had been ripped from his chest. "I sold Pop's bike."

He couldn't decide if he should be miserable or doing cartwheels at the moment.

"Why?" Quinn grabbed the phone. "Call him back. Tell him the deal's off. I've got this. You don't have to give up the Indian to save Devra. I'll cover the legal fees, assuming we can get things straightened out tomorrow."

"She's my wife. I can take care of her." Trevon tried not to be insulted. He knew Quinn was only attempting to help, but at some point he wanted to be able to provide for the woman he loved. Hell, for the man he loved, too. Even if Quinn didn't need his assistance now, he might someday.

Quinn backed up a step and then another. He'd already been on the verge of a meltdown when he'd left earlier. It looked like Trevon had unintentionally triggered him, shoving him into an abyss filled with bad memories and emotional scars. "I guess you're right. It was wrong of me to assume I had any claim over either of you. You're married. I'm just the guy you fuck on the side."

"What the hell did you say?" *Oh shit.* Now they'd done it. Devra must have heard them shouting and run over from the cottage. She prowled toward them with her hands on her hips. She might have been small, but she was no one to mess around with.

Trevon felt like he needed to fix things before they got even more out of control. "Devra, calm down. It's my fault. I keep fucking up. I didn't mean it like that, Quinn. Not at all. It's just that I caused all of this. I put Devra in this situation because I messed up her application."

Of course Devra and Quinn both rushed to reassure him. Except then Quinn stopped short of telling him everything would be fine.

"Guys." Quinn cleared his throat. "I have some bad news. It's worse than the simple stuff."

He straightened his spine, then told them the facts about what Agent Mikalski had discovered and the fraud claims that had been filed against Devra.

"So it really was because of me." Trevon doubled over clutching his knees. "I was curious. If she hadn't been generous and willing to experiment so that I would finally know for sure...none of this would have happened."

Devra gasped. "Trevon, that's ridiculous. This all started because I couldn't handle feeling useless and I was too afraid to ask for what I wanted—you. As my husband, in every sense of the word. Along the way I discovered something I needed that I hadn't even known about before. At the end of the day, nothing we've done is wrong. Nothing violates the intent of the law. It's just not written for people like us."

"Agent Mikalski said that right there is your best argument at your interview. You'll have to convince them that we have something special. Something equal to a traditional marriage. Something that's not sordid or clandestine. They'll need to understand that Trevon is aware and onboard with it."

"That won't be hard. Each of us has made sacrifices and mistakes. And we're all willing to give each other grace and forgiveness at our own expense." Devra smiled at Trevon and Quinn. "That's how I know for sure."

"Know what?" Quinn asked.

"That we love each other." Despite the gravity of the situation, her smile outshone the stars beginning to twinkle overhead.

"I do," Quinn promised, and held his hands out to them. "I love you both."

"Same." Trevon took Quinn's hand and held his out to Devra.

"Not only do I love you both, but I'm *in love* with you, too." Devra sighed. "That's not something I thought I'd be lucky enough to experience once, never mind twice, in my lifetime. So even if it was only for a little while, I'm grateful."

She took their hands, completing the circle.

"If it has to be that way...if they make you leave, I'll come with you," Trevon told her. "You're not going to be on your own again."

Quinn made an *oomph* sound as if someone had punched him in the stomach.

Trevon wondered if Quinn would be able to walk away from Hot Rides, Hot Rods, and the only family that had ever stood by him to chase Devra and Trevon halfway around the world. He was noble enough to try it. Except Trevon knew that whether he stayed or followed, he'd always be torn in two.

Besides, Devra wasn't having any of that anyway. "No. Trevon, promise you won't. Look what happened to my father. He was far less controversial than you would be in my society. No. Quinn needs you. And we promised we'd never leave him. If I can't keep my word, I want you to do it for me. It will make things bearable if I'm sure the two of you are happy and together."

Trevon started to argue. Quinn stopped him and said, "We're not going to agree on this. So let's hope it doesn't come to that. I don't want to waste tonight fighting. I'd rather spend it loving you both."

Trevon could agree to that.

So they did.

28

Quinn, Trevon, and Devra stood down the street from the government building in the next larger city over from Middletown. The guys were dressed in suits they'd had to borrow from friends, since they figured ripped jeans and oil-stained shirts probably wouldn't help them appear more respectable than they actually were, while Devra wore a simple, modest black dress. She'd pulled her hair up into a bun and applied enough neutral-toned makeup to feel at her best without going over the top and looking too done up.

It was absolutely crazy to her that someone's first impression of them might determine the entire course of her future. But that was a reality they had to face.

Mr. Ribold, the immigration lawyer Alanso had recommended and Trevon had retained, trailed a few steps behind them. He kind of frightened her, which she figured was a good thing in this situation. He was stern, direct, and intelligent.

Mr. Ribold had been briefed, and though he wasn't

sure how much he could assist, he'd agreed to come with them that morning. He damn well better, since Trevon had already sacrificed Pop's bike for the man's help.

It was another weight added to her growing burden of guilt. She was hurting people she loved just by being. She had nothing to do with the war raging in her country, yet the evil tendrils radiating out from the conflict were wrapping around even more blameless people here and pulling them into the trouble as surely as they'd ensnared her father.

Devra clutched her stomach, then smoothed out her dress for the thousandth time.

Two minutes early, Agent Mikalski appeared at their meeting point. He introduced himself to Devra, Trevon, and their lawyer, shaking their hands. "Are you ready for this?"

"No." She bit her lip. "But I'm prepared to lay myself bare and hope it's enough."

"Should Trevon and I stay with you guys or wait outside?" Quinn asked.

"What do you want to get out of today?" Agent Mikalski stared at Quinn, as if telling him not to be stupid.

"I want to show whoever determines what happens to my family that we are in a committed, loving relationship, even if that doesn't look like an old-fashioned, government-recognized marriage. I'll do anything to reduce the risk of Devra being deported. I love her and Trevon."

Devra and Trevon smiled warmly, first at each other, then at Quinn. Devra said, "That's what we want, too. Please let them come with me. If I have to go...I want to spend every last minute with them I can."

"And if the decision is to send you away?" Agent

Mikalski asked, and Devra got the feeling it was some sort of test. She didn't blame him for his mini-interrogation. After all, it was his ass—and career—on the line, too.

"Then at least I know they'll have each other. It's most important to me that they're okay." Devra sniffed. "I'll be fine."

Judging by their deadpan faces, they all knew that was a lie. Both because her heart would never recover and because her country would be a toxic environment for her, especially if any hint of why she'd been deported was to be leaked. She wouldn't last long back home.

"I haven't known your lovers long," Agent Mikalski told Quinn. "But seeing you like this, having these discussions, is telling me everything I need to know. I took this job to be on the side of what's right, and today I believe that's keeping you together. So I'll do what I can. Like I told you before, the best shot you have is to be completely honest and open. Let everyone who doubts your story see what I see right now."

Quinn drew a deep breath then exhaled. He took Devra's hand in one of his and Trevon's in the other. Together, they walked toward the monolithic marble building where their fate would be decided by strangers while Mr. Ribold marched one step behind, straightening his tie as if he was adjusting his armor for battle.

"I'll see you inside," Agent Mikalski said, then disappeared.

"He's a little too good at that," Devra said under her breath.

When they reached the door, their lawyer held it open and ushered them inside. Devra shivered. Not only because of the overpowering air-conditioning and clinical, artificial light that wiped out the effects of the sunshine on her skin either.

"We can do this," Quinn said to no one in particular, probably trying to convince himself more than her and Trevon.

After they went to the front desk, they were directed to a no-frills waiting room where the forty-five minutes they were delayed seemed like an eternity. Trevon tapped his toe, Quinn drummed his fingers on his leg, and Devra tried to look nonchalant when every instinct in her was screaming at her to flee.

"Mrs. Russell?" a woman asked from the entry to a long interior hallway.

Devra stood, and her guys did, too. They flanked her as they approached the stern woman. Devra smiled and said hello, but the woman didn't respond. Instead, she motioned for Devra, Quinn, Trevon, and Mr. Ribold to follow her down the windowless corridor.

They were shown into a bland beige room with a single crappy conference table and a one-way mirror on the wall. Though she hadn't heard the door lock behind the woman who'd showed them in, Devra already felt like she was being held against her will. The walls closed in around her.

Devra couldn't wait for Agent Mikalski to come through the door. At least then she'd feel like they had someone on their side.

Except when someone did join them—after another interminable half hour—it wasn't Agent Mikalski.

It was a balding man in an ill-fitting suit with a red tie that looked like it had been cinched too tight, putting his head in danger of popping right off. He hardly glanced at them as he mumbled his name, Agent

Donaldson, before plopping into a chair across from them.

He opened a folder and sifted through a few papers. One was a full-sheet copy of the picture of her and Quinn kissing. Another seemed to be a long letter, probably the complaint about her working at Hot Rides.

For a moment, Devra wished Quinn and Trevon hadn't talked back to that hateful bully that day. Except she knew combating stereotypes and preconceived notions—about her homeland, her customs, and just plain her—would be something she had to deal with for the rest of the time she spent in Quinn and Trevon's world.

Right now, she was growing more and more certain that might only be another five minutes. Her throat felt like it was closing and it was getting difficult to breathe the stale air, which stung her throat.

Quinn looked to Mr. Ribold, who shook his head no, indicating they shouldn't offer any excuses or talk before being asked direct questions. Devra felt like her neck was resting in a guillotine and she was waiting for the blade to drop.

"Mrs. Russell, it seems we've invited you in today to discuss some information we've received that questions the validity of your marriage as well as testimony that you're doing unauthorized work in this country." Agent Donaldson droned on, as if he was only seeing the ink on the papers and not the living, breathing people in front of him.

Devra looked at Trevon, memorizing every detail of him, and then she did the same to Quinn. This was going to be goodbye.

"My client has not taken payment for any labor that

violates her status." Mr. Ribold translated her actions into legal jargon. "She has, on occasion, provided uncompensated assistance that would not constitute formal employment and she will not be doing so again from this point forward."

The agent grunted without even looking up from his folder. "Would you like to address the allegations of fraud relating to your marriage with Mr. Russell?" Agent Donaldson asked, this time meeting her gaze for a fleeting pass.

"I would yes," she said when Mr. Ribold began to reply for her. Like Agent Mikalski said, the only shot she had was to make this jaded bureaucrat understand what it was like to be her and to be in love, equally, with two people who complemented each other and made her life whole.

"Go ahead."

"I love Trevon. Our marriage is true in every sense." Ironically, it hadn't been until they'd met Quinn. He was the thing that had bonded them, not broken them. She paused to look over at her husband, who smiled back at her, encouraging her to go on.

"Then would you care to explain this?" The man placed the photo on the table and spun it toward her. "I tend to think it's pretty undeniable evidence, especially since you've brought this man with you here today."

"It's proof that I am capable of loving more than one person. A fact my husband understands and supports, as he also loves Quinn." Devra sat straighter, daring the man to say it was untrue. He could have no ammunition against her statements because they were completely honest and accurate. The truth was her best and only defense.

Mr. Ribold added on, "Recent changes to LGBTQ

status recognition have set precedents that support the acceptance of non-traditional definitions of marriage. In this case, my client and her husband are engaged in a polyamorous relationship that includes Mr. Daily but does not detract from the sanctity of their marriage. Rather, it enhances it."

"Is that true?" Agent Donaldson asked Trevon.

"Absolutely. Devra has never been unfaithful and our marriage is no sham. We love and support each other, including in our joint pursuit of Quinn." Trevon leaned forward then and laid everything on the table, his heart included. "If you take Devra from me...from us...it will destroy us. We are upholding the spirit of the law by living —and loving—together, working to build a better life for the three of us in this country we love."

The agent made a few notes on the inside of the folder. He stood, tucking it beneath his arm. "I'm going to have to review this case with my boss, who is currently out to lunch. Until we can make a decision, I'd like to ask that Mrs. Russell come with me to a holding area. The rest of you may go."

"We're not leaving her here in some glorified jail cell." Quinn stood, planting his hands on the table. "She's not a criminal or an animal. She hasn't done anything wrong!"

Mr. Ribold stood, too, telling Quinn to calm down and take his seat, which did no good whatsoever.

"That's not your decision to make, Mr. Daily." The man tipped his chin up as if he enjoyed wielding what power he had over people he considered lesser-thans.

"You're tearing lives apart!" Trevon held his hands out, palms up. "Can't you see that?"

"I'm doing my job. Following the rules, as you should have." Agent Donaldson tucked the folder closer to his chest. "The evidence in this case is straightforward."

Devra could see his mind was already made up.

She was leaving.

Forever.

She got to her feet, too, tugging on Quinn's arm until he turned toward her and clutched her to him as if she was a life ring and he was drowning. Trevon did the same from behind her.

"I don't want our last moments together to be ugly ones," Devra whispered.

While the guys were trying to comfort her, Devra was doing the same for her men.

She turned and dragged Trevon down for one, sweet, lingering kiss and a few whispered words. From him, promising she would be okay and they would sort things out. From her, telling him that he'd already given her a lifetime of happiness rolled into the short time they'd shared.

Then she turned to Quinn and did the same. She told him how much he'd impacted her life for the better and that she'd never forget what he'd done for them.

It wasn't nearly long enough to express to her two lovers everything she had in her heart, but it was all the time she would get to try.

"Mrs. Russell, this way, please." Agent Donaldson stood by the door and held his hand out, indicating she should walk deeper into the belly of the building, away from freedom.

She couldn't help looking over her shoulder a hundred times at Quinn and Trevon, who were standing in the hallway, defeated, shoulders slumped, watching her go.

Every step she put between them felt like a hundred miles.

Devra was still in shock when Agent Donaldson stuck her in a tiny room, hardly bigger than a closet, with a reinforced metal door. What was she, some kind of superhero who could escape a place like this?

She wrapped her fingers around the cold metal, wondering how long she'd have to stay penned in. Already, she thought the confinement might drive her mad.

There were no clocks and no windows. No way to tell how long it had been other than to count the seconds. When she got bored enough, Devra did exactly that. She made it over five thousand before a very ordinary woman came down the outside hall, then peered inside Devra's cubby.

"You understand how fucked you are, right?" the woman asked.

"Yes." Devra didn't see any reason to deny it.

"So don't you dare take this for granted. And be more discreet in the future, please." The woman opened the door, making Devra feel ten times lighter than she had while wondering if she would rot in there.

"I'm free to go?" Devra asked, even though it sounded like a pipe dream.

The woman smiled then. "It seems *someone* accidentally deleted the emails containing the evidence and complaints against you and the originals were prematurely shredded. Since they don't exist, there's nothing we can do about them."

Thank God for Agent Mikalski. He'd come through for them. Devra wondered if he'd been busy taking care of those things while his colleague was interrogating her. It was kind of genius.

She'd have to remember to give him the biggest hug imaginable next time she saw him. In private, of course. They were going to have to be a lot more subtle about stuff like that from now on.

Devra couldn't believe it. She was going to walk out of this hellhole.

"Do me one other favor?" the woman asked.

"What?" Devra would do just about anything.

"Tell Kaelyn at Hot Rods that Amanda says hi. Tell her I came down with a sudden case of look-the-other-way because I want to make up for some of the damage our fathers, their antiquated beliefs, and their political positions have done, including to her. I always felt bad about it. She's a decent person."

"Ummm, I'll try to remember all that." Devra was having trouble processing anything except the prospect of freedom at the moment.

The woman shrugged. "We've all got our struggles. Now get the hell out of here so you have one fewer to deal with. Take this too."

She held out a small envelope to Devra, who clasped it in her trembling hands. "What is it?"

"Your status change documents and your green card. *Someone* told me to put a rush on them, and hopes you'll forgive him or her for being absent. This was the only way he or she could think of to definitively protect you."

"Thank you," Devra whispered, staring in awe.

"You're welcome. Even if you have scooped up *two* of the most eligible bachelors in Middletown for yourself." The woman grinned then. It completely transformed her face.

This still wasn't coffee talk or time to make a new bestie.

"Can I go now?" Devra asked, her skin crawling at her confinement even though she was grateful for this woman's moral compass and her need to give her opponents the finger.

"Yeah. I'm going to walk you out. If we pass anyone in the halls, don't make eye contact and definitely do not respond to any snide comments or derogatory remarks that are made. Do not give them one single reason to put you back in here. If you do, it will be impossible for me or anyone else to get you out again."

"I understand."

Amanda stood and marched Devra to the front door of the building, ensuring no one harassed her before she could become a free woman again.

She set her stare on the final turn that would take her to the lobby.

Devra had one goal in mind—find her guys and make sure they could never be torn apart as they'd almost been that day.

29

Devra didn't care about acting poised. She wasn't.

She smacked the bar on the front door and flung it open. That first breath of fresh air and the sunlight that fell on her face made her sure she never wanted to go back to being imprisoned—by her own beliefs, by her fears, by the opinions of others or by any government—ever again.

She made a run for it. Without knowing where to go or how to get home, she ran.

Devra sprinted across the stone courtyard and saw familiar faces. She headed toward them, ready to throw herself into Trevon and Quinn's arms, except they were...arguing?

What the hell? It was her worst nightmare. That they wouldn't survive on their own. For a moment, she had a vision of what their lives might have been like if the past half hour had gone differently. She swore to make sure that never happened.

Together, they would be perfectly balanced, and too strong to tear down.

"Guys!" she shouted. They froze, then turned as one toward her.

Their eyes lit up and their faces morphed from masks of rage and grief into ones of unadulterated joy. It was about that time that she flung herself toward them, knowing full well they would catch her.

They did, surrounding her with their heat and strength.

"Devra! What happened?" Trevon asked, his hands shaking as they rubbed over her back in endless circuits.

"Agent Mikalski came through for us. But...it was close. Scary there for a few minutes." She looked over her shoulder as if Agent Donaldson could be trailing her, ready to drag her back inside kicking and screaming, away from the two loves of her life. "Can we get out of here?"

Quinn was already escorting them toward the spot where his brother's Barracuda was waiting. They said their thanks and goodbyes to Mr. Ribold then piled inside the flashy purple car and headed...home.

Devra buried her face against Trevon's ribs and let her tears fall silently. She couldn't wait to show them what she had realized in that holding cell. That if she got out and had a chance to see them again, that she wouldn't go a single day more without telling them, and showing them exactly how much she loved them both.

Devra didn't remember anything about the long ride home from the Immigration office except the weight and strength of Trevon's arms around her and Quinn telling them over and over how thankful he was to have them in his life and that he'd never take them for granted.

They made one relatively short stop at Hot Rods to

share their unbelievable news with Quinn's family, who were starting to feel like Trevon and Devra's family, too. After a few tears and lots of congratulations and even some laughter over the guys and what they looked like wearing suits, they left with promises to return—all three of them—for Sunday night dinner that week and every week after for the foreseeable future.

When they walked into Quinn's house, their shared home, Devra didn't even hesitate.

She stripped off her dress and dropped it on the floor as she headed straight for their bedroom.

Behind her, she heard her men whispering, wondering if she needed space or...them.

"I wasn't planning on taking a nap," Devra called. "Who's joining me? Or should I take care of myself in here?"

Not three seconds later, she was bounced and jostled as the two large men raced each other to her then hit the mattress hard. They sandwiched her between them, making her feel warm and protected, completely loved.

Because she was.

They took turns kissing each other in every combination. Devra was grateful for the time Quinn and Trevon spent making out because it gave her time to catch her breath. Time to appreciate how gorgeous they were, too.

Sex with them was a blend of playful romance that she would never get tired of.

But Quinn was dead serious when he rolled her onto her back, spread her legs, and fit his cock to her pussy. She ran her hands down his tattooed chest, loving the way he'd chosen to decorate his skin.

Meanwhile, Trevon knelt nearby. He seemed to love

watching Quinn pleasure his wife nearly as much as he got off on doing it himself sometimes. Devra was fine with that.

She reached out and wrapped her hand around his impressive cock, beginning to stroke him in time to Quinn's forward motions. It was like he was fucking them both through her.

"Soon he's going to be here, doing what I'm doing," Quinn told her. "Why don't you suck him? Get him good and hard so he's ready when I want him in place."

Devra opened her mouth and Trevon didn't hesitate to feed her his growing erection. He was so big that she didn't always do a very good job at swallowing him, but she made up for it by licking and sucking on the tip where he liked it best anyway. Quinn was even better at it than her, though.

"Can I have a taste?" He nudged her chin away so that he could take Trevon between his lips even as he began to fuck her harder.

Devra caressed his back with one hand, urging him on. The other she used to rub up Trevon's thigh and ass. He was rocking forward, fucking Quinn's mouth even as Quinn fucked Devra's pussy.

She loved to watch the men please each other.

It didn't take long before she was ready to come. Quinn must have felt her tightening around him and moved faster, harder between her thighs, giving her the extra push she needed.

As she was flying, he withdrew, instructing Trevon to take his place.

Trevon was bigger. He stretched her open again as he worked inside her carefully, with more smoothness and finesse than Quinn had taken her with. But not for long.

Because once he'd caught his breath and gotten himself under control, Quinn slapped Trevon's ass, then growled, "That's right, fuck her good."

Trevon jerked, embedding himself deeper in Devra than he normally went. She moaned and ground on him, impaling herself even further.

"Don't you dare shoot yet," Quinn warned Trevon. "Please your wife. Make her come around you, too. And if you do, we're going to try something new. I'm going to be in the middle of you both. I want you to fuck me tonight, Trevon. Is that something you'd be into?"

"Hell, yes." Trevon growled. His eyes shined bright as he applied himself to bringing Devra as much pleasure as he could.

Devra lifted her head and kissed Trevon, helping him concentrate so that he could have what she knew he yearned for. The sooner she got off, the sooner they'd all be connected.

"Then," Quinn told them, "We're going to come together. All of us."

That had happened naturally a couple times, but not usually. Devra admitted she loved it when it had. For all of them to be so in sync and riding the high together before melting into a heap of snuggles. Yeah, she treasured that. This time more than ever, she needed it.

So she helped Trevon out by sliding her hand down the center of her body and rubbing her clit while her husband made love to her.

"Very nice," Quinn praised them both as he observed their intimacy. It had never been as powerful as what they shared today. "This is how you're going to spend every day for the rest of your lives. Living and loving together."

That's all it took. Devra lost it.

She arched tight like a coiled spring before her orgasm released the tension in her body all at once. She came so hard around Trevon that she was afraid he might break Quinn's rules and flood her pussy at the same time.

But Quinn was smarter than that.

He distracted Trevon by showing him what he'd been doing while they fucked. Devra hadn't seen him grab it, but he'd used one of the toys she'd seen in his drawer the day she'd retrieved his lube to prepare himself for Trevon. His ass was going to need all the help he could get.

Trevon was harder than she'd ever seen him, and that was saying something.

"I'm ready for you, Trevon," he promised. "I'm ready to be yours as much as you're mine, and for us both to be Devra's."

"Are you good with that, too?" Trevon asked Devra with one final kiss as he slipped from her still-clenching channel.

"Of course." She reached up to stroke his cheek. "Make him ours. Show him that he's not on the outside anymore."

Quinn cried out as Trevon reached for him and their mouths clashed. While they kissed furiously, Trevon removed the plug from Quinn's prepared ass and urged him to take his place in the cradle of Devra's thighs.

She sighed as he settled in, right where he belonged. Almost. "Quinn, I want you inside me when he joins with you."

"You just came." He kissed her cheeks softly. "If you hold me while he makes love to me, that'll be enough."

"Not for me." She reached between them and guided him home.

They both gasped.

Devra ran her hands all over his powerful shoulders and down his arms. She would never get enough of either of her men. She distracted him as Trevon prepared his shaft, using extra lubrication despite Quinn's forethought.

"Just do it, Trevon." Quinn urged, showing them that simply because he was the man in the middle, didn't mean he wasn't the one running the show. "You're not going to hurt me. It's so much more painful being apart than it ever could being together."

Devra's husband grimaced at that. After today, each of them couldn't deny it was true.

"Go ahead, Trevon. Give it to him," she encouraged her husband as Quinn's cock twitched deep inside her. "I promise you, he wants this."

Trevon looked between Devra and Quinn twice, then he took his cock in his fist and lined it up with Quinn's ass. It took him a few tries, but eventually, he grunted and Quinn cursed.

Devra kissed Quinn gently, soothingly, helping him ride out those first few moments of discomfort. She grabbed his ass and spread him wide to give Trevon's fat shaft room to penetrate.

All the while, she stared into Quinn's beautiful blue eyes, letting him see how much she admired him for allowing himself to be completely open to them and the possibility of getting wrecked. Not physically, but so much deeper than that.

Finally, he was giving them everything and holding nothing in reserve.

He trusted them never to forsake him. As he should.

Any slight pain seemed to help him regain control. He stepped away from the edge of climax long enough to enjoy what Trevon was giving him.

At first it was only Trevon's slow, languid motions shuttling Quinn in and out of Devra's pussy, which reawakened gradually. Over time, Quinn could no longer remain passive. He began to move, retreating from her a tiny bit to swallow more of Trevon's cock, then advancing to bury himself in her body again and again. Back and forth, he found pleasure in both directions.

"I can't do this for long," Trevon groaned as a warning. "You feel too good, Quinn, and you look so sexy fucking my wife. Making her moan and sigh like that. Damn."

"Same," Devra agreed. Already, her desire was ramping up again, making her eager to crest the wave and surf down the rapture with them.

"I could do it all night." Quinn grinned. "I've always been one for a wild ride."

Right then, Trevon gave him what he asked for. He gripped Quinn's hips and began to fuck mercilessly. Quinn must have clenched around Trevon, who shouted their names.

Devra caved. She called it for both men since they seemed unwilling to be the one to end their mutual rapture. "Enough. Enough waiting. I want us to share this. Come, together. Now!"

They were frenzied for a moment, each of them trying to get as much as they could of the two others. But eventually it was too much. Trevon bypassed Quinn's head to kiss Devra. He stared deep into her eyes and let go, pumping Quinn full of his semen. The first splash of Quinn's hot come in her pussy triggered her own orgasm. She milked him dry with the clenching of her muscles.

He glided as deep as he could inside Devra's pussy and unloaded, pouring every drop of himself into her even as Trevon did the same to Quinn. Devra and Trevon smothered him, hugging him from both sides, taking complete satisfaction from the man they shared equally.

Several minutes later, when they had untangled their limbs and resettled themselves, with Devra in the middle and both men cuddled up against her, pillowing their heads on her breasts, she knew this was how their lives were meant to be.

There were so many things she wanted to say, but she settled for, "I love you guys more than you'll ever know."

Trevon kissed her cheek and Quinn kissed the other. Trevon said, "I have some idea, because I love you both the same way."

Quinn stared at them for a while, as if he finally believed that they were his and he was theirs and that no one was going anywhere. Not tonight and not ever.

"I love you, too. Wherever fate carries us, I'll follow. If something pulls us apart, I will always come back for you two." They were simple words, but a promise, too. One that Devra recognized as his ultimate standard of loyalty and love. Because it was what Roman had done for Quinn, the one act that saved his life and put him on the path to finding this everlasting happiness they now shared.

"I'll always come back for you, too," she responded in kind, letting him know that she got him. She understood.

"I don't plan to be more than a dick's length away from either of you again, but...if worst comes to worst..." Trevon nodded. "I'll always come back for you."

30

Agent Jordan Mikalski stood quietly near the back row of folding chairs set up on the lawn of Hot Rides while Quinn, Trevon, and Devra exchanged vows. Devra was dressed in an exquisite traditional outfit of red silk ornately embroidered with gold thread. Her eyes were darkly lined, and elaborate gold jewelry draped her face, including a chain that ran through a sparkling nose ring.

Trevon and Quinn had damn near fallen over themselves when they caught sight of her coming to claim them in front of the dozens of friends who had gathered to witness the occasion. Jordan had already met an entire construction crew, plus gotten to know a bunch of the Hot Rods mechanics better.

Then of course, there was the one person he was dying to talk to, who kept avoiding him. Wren must have been as aware of him as he was of her to dodge every single one of his attempts.

After the simple ceremony had concluded, Jordan took his turn in the crowd of people waiting to offer their congratulations. While he was standing there, a cheer went up from the people closest to the happy trio.

He saw why when Gavyn wheeled out an antique Indian Chief motorcycle that looked like it had been meticulously restored and handed it to Trevon. Jordan edged closer to hear what the commotion was all about and found himself standing next to a short guy with dark hair.

"What's going on?" Jordan asked.

"Gavyn bought back Trevon's grandfather's motorcycle. The one he sold to pay for Devra's legal fees, college tuition, and a down payment on that empty restaurant on Third Street." The guy turned and thrust out his hand. "I'm Ollie, by the way. I helped broker the deal. I felt like shit about it, too. This is...perfect."

Jordan wondered what it would be like to belong to a network of friends and lovers like the one these three fortunate people had. To cover up the intensity of the moment, Gavyn joked around. "Consider it your Christmas bonus for the next fifty years you work at Hot Rides."

Jordan didn't have to be an expert at reading people to see how touched Trevon, Devra, and Quinn were that the Hot Rides founder would do something so monumental for them.

Gavyn clapped Trevon on the back, then kissed Devra's temple. "Welcome to the family."

"Hey, what about me?" Quinn reached for his friend and smothered him in a bear hug.

"We've been family for a while now." Gavyn ruffled Quinn's hair.

"Hey, don't mess him up. We haven't taken pictures yet." Sally waved her camera at Gavyn and Quinn.

While they wandered off, Jordan let his eyes roam around the clearing. There were couples and groups all around him. It became easy to pick out those who were together. Those who had a bond that went beyond basic friendship.

"I think we might be the odd men out here," Ollie said with a snort. "You know most of them share their lovers?"

Jordan nodded. "They're lucky bastards."

"You're into that, too?" Ollie asked. "Maybe I need to give it a try. Not having a lot of luck finding a woman on my own."

"With the right person, it could be life altering." His gaze locked on Wren as her laugh rang out. Never would get tired of hearing that sound. Never could take his eyes off her either.

"Her?" Ollie leaned in. "She doesn't seem like the type."

"There's a type?" Jordan hoped the guy got the hint and backed off Wren. He didn't like other men thinking of her in bed. Not that they could imagine how spectacular she was when she let passion consume her.

"Well, I mean, she looks so sophisticated and maybe a little uptight. Not someone I'd imagine cutting loose with one guy, never mind two."

"You'd be surprised." Jordan wished like hell this wasn't a dry wedding. He could have used a flute or twelve of champagne right then. "I've been in love with her for nearly ten years. That image she puts out there, it's a front. It keeps her from getting hurt. On the inside, she's...everything."

"Then what the hell are you doing over here talking to me when you could be dancing with her?"

"Pretty sure she hates my guts." Jordan stifled a groan.

"How do you know? It's probably not that bad." Ollie elbowed the agent in the ribs.

"Oh yeah? Watch this." Jordan waited until the next time Wren's light gray eyes flicked to his, because they always did. She was as aware of him as he was of her. The pull between them was irresistible, at least for him. She seemed to do a fine job of shutting it down.

When they did, he lifted his very non-alcoholic drink in a long distance toast.

She responded by giving him the finger, flinging her platinum hair over her shoulder, then spinning on her mile-high stilettos and marching off in the opposite direction.

"Oh, yup. You're fucked." Ollie winced. "Sorry, bud. What'd you do to piss her off?"

Got her soulmate killed. Even seltzer churned in his gut like too much whiskey then. "Doesn't matter. There's no hope."

"That's rough. I'm sorry. But in that case...do you mind if I go introduce myself to her?" Ollie wondered.

"Be aware that if you hurt her, I know a million ways to make a body disappear and have friends in every police force in the country."

"Noted." Ollie drained his own glass then clapped his hand on Jordan's shoulder. "I'll put in a good word for you."

"Don't. Not if you want any chance with her." Jordan was resigned to the fact that Wren would take other lovers. She'd done some wild things since they'd been apart. Ones that terrified him and made him pretty sure she was trying hard to scrub memories of their times together from her mind no matter the cost. At least Ollie was someone Quinn and Gavyn knew and trusted enough to invite into their shop.

If Jordan couldn't take care of her, then he wanted someone else to do it for him.

Even if it caused even more damage to his already tattered soul.

———

Don't miss Wren and Jordan's story in Slow Ride (Powertools: Hot Rides, Book 2), available HERE.

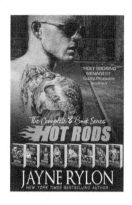

If you missed out on the Powertools: Hot Rods series, you can buy all eight books in a discounted single-volume boxset by clicking HERE.

If you'd like to start at the very beginning with the Powertools Crew, you can download a discounted boxset of the first six books HERE. Yes, know it says complete series but I wrote a seventh book more recently and haven't gotten around to updating the boxset yet, sorry! You can find the seventh Powertools book, More the Merrier, HERE.

CLAIM A $5 GIFT CERTIFICATE

Jayne is so sure you will love her books, she'd like you to try any one of your choosing for free. Claim your $5 gift certificate by signing up for her newsletter. You'll also learn about freebies, new releases, extras, appearances, and more!

www.jaynerylon.com/newsletter

WHAT WAS YOUR FAVORITE PART?

Did you enjoy this book? If so, please leave a review and tell your friends about it. Word of mouth and online reviews are immensely helpful and greatly appreciated.

JAYNE'S SHOP

Check out Jayne's online shop for autographed print books, direct download ebooks, reading-themed apparel up to size 5XL, mugs, tote bags, notebooks, Mr. Rylon's wood (you'll have to see it for yourself!) and more.
www.jaynerylon.com/shop

LISTEN UP!

The majority of Jayne's books are also available in audio format on Audible, Amazon and iTunes.

ABOUT THE AUTHOR

 Jayne Rylon is a *New York Times* and *USA Today* bestselling author who has sold more than one million books. She has received numerous industry awards including the Romantic Times Reviewers' Choice Award for Best Indie Erotic Romance and the Swirl Award, which recognizes excellence in diverse romance. She is an Honor Roll member of the Romance Writers of America. Her stories used to begin as daydreams in seemingly endless business meetings, but now she is a full time author, who employs the skills she learned from her straight-laced corporate existence in the business of writing. She lives in Ohio with her husband, the infamous Mr. Rylon, and their cat, Frodo. When she can escape her purple office, she loves to travel the world, avoid speeding tickets in her beloved Sky, SCUBA dive, hunt Pokemon, and–of course–read.

Jayne Loves To Hear From Readers
www.jaynerylon.com
contact@jaynerylon.com
PO Box 10, Pickerington, OH 43147

facebook.com/jaynerylon

twitter.com/JayneRylon

instagram.com/jaynerylon

youtube.com/jaynerylonbooks

bookbub.com/profile/jayne-rylon

amazon.com/author/jaynerylon

ALSO BY JAYNE RYLON

4-EVER

A New Adult Reverse Harem Series

4-Ever Theirs

4-Ever Mine

EVER AFTER DUET

Reverse Harem Featuring Characters From The 4-Ever Series

Fourplay

Fourkeeps

POWERTOOLS

Five Guys Who Get It On With Each Other & One Girl. Enough Said?

Kate's Crew

Morgan's Surprise

Kayla's Gift

Devon's Pair

Nailed to the Wall

Hammer it Home

More the Merrier *NEW*

HOT RODS

Powertools Spin Off. Keep up with the Crew plus...

Seven Guys & One Girl. Enough Said?

King Cobra

Mustang Sally

Super Nova

Rebel on the Run

Swinger Style

Barracuda's Heart

Touch of Amber

Long Time Coming

HOT RIDES

Powertools and Hot Rods Spin Off.

Menage and Motorcycles

Wild Ride

Slow Ride

Rough Ride - Coming Soon!

Joy Ride - Coming Soon!

Hard Ride - Coming Soon!

MEN IN BLUE

Hot Cops Save Women In Danger

Night is Darkest

Razor's Edge

Mistress's Master

Spread Your Wings

Wounded Hearts

Bound For You

DIVEMASTERS

PARANORMALS

Vampires, Witches, And A Man Trapped In A Painting

Paranormal Double Pack Boxset

Picture Perfect

Reborn

PENTHOUSE PLEASURES

Naughty Manhattanite Neighbors Find Kinky Love

Taboo

Kinky

Sinner

ROAMING WITH THE RYLONS

Non-fiction Travelogues about Jayne & Mr. Rylon's Adventures

Australia and New Zealand

Made in the USA
Las Vegas, NV
24 February 2021

18496006R00164